MISTLETOE

LYN GARDNER

Edited by Bron T.
Cover by Robin Ludwig Design Inc.
http://www.gobookcoverdesign.com

Library of Congress Number: 2014933408

ISBN 13: 978-1519261601
ISBN-10: 1519261608

To GG
Who carried Christmas in her heart all year long.
May we all have learned from you.

ACKNOWLEDGMENTS

I would like to thank my friend, beta, editor and confidant, Bron, for all her hard work on this book. Through all the edits and the arguments, you were always there for me.

A tremendously large "thank you" goes out to all the readers. Your reviews have brought attention to my words, and your letters have brought a smile to my face. I know I have a long way to go, and I know I have a lot to learn, but by your comments, I think I'm on the right track.

And finally to Nikki, my very first beta, whose encouragement kept me grounded when those around me tried to bring me down. I hope you realize that this would have never happened if you hadn't answered my request for a beta a few years ago. I have a feeling that you may be smiling right now, RC, and if truth be known...so am I.

CHAPTER ONE

"You need to eat more."

Letting out a hearty laugh, he rubbed his rounded belly and grinned at his wife. "You say that every year."

Smiling back at her husband, she said, "True, but you know how you get this time of the year. You're so busy answering all those letters, that you forget to eat, and you know you need all the insulation you can get."

"Well, if I get any more insulated, we're going to have to add another reindeer to the sleigh to get it off the ground," Kris Kringle said as he brushed a few crumbs off his long, white beard.

"Santa! Santa! Santa!" Percy Giggly-Legs cried out as he ran down the long hallway leading from the stables to the main dining room. "Santa! Santa! Santa!"

Startled, Kris Kringle turned in his chair. "Percy, what is all the commotion about?"

Coming to a sliding stop when he reached the head of the table, the little elf held his hand to his chest as he tried to catch his breath. After a few moments, he shoved a piece of paper into Santa's hand. "I was cleaning out some of the old sacks when I found that," Percy said. "I'm sorry. I don't know how it was missed."

"Missed?" Santa said, looking at the crinkled piece of notepaper in his hand. "Percy, if this is a child's wish, we have plenty of time. Christmas isn't for another twenty-three days."

Penitent, Percy hung his head and said quietly, "I'm afraid we're a little late on that one, sir."

Cocking his head to the side, Santa glanced first at Mrs. Claus and then slowly unfolded the letter. Seeing the date on the top of the page, his eyes flew open wide. Quickly scanning the words, Santa looked over the top of his glasses and glared at his lead elf. "Percy Giggly-Legs, how could you let this happen?"

"I'm sorry, sir, but it got stuck in the lining of one of the old sacks."

"In the lining, you say?" Santa said, reading the date on the letter again. Looking up, he sighed. "Oh my."

"Poppa, what seems to be the problem?" Mrs. Claus asked, seeing the frown on the chubby man's face.

"It seems that a little girl made a wish thirty years ago that we never granted."

"What?" she exclaimed, jumping out of her chair. Snatching the letter from Santa's hand, Mrs. Claus read the words written in a child's scrawl. It only took a few moments, but by the time she returned the letter to Santa, her cheeks were the color of Rudolph's nose. Casting a quick scowl in Percy's direction, Mrs. Claus waddled as fast as her tubbiness would allow across the room to the two digital counters hanging on the wall. Although each displayed an identical number over a dozen digits long, with the letter now in Santa's hand, they all watched in horror as the red counter on the top grew by one number, but the green counter below it remained unchanged.

"Percy, do you see what you've done?" Mrs. Claus said, pointing at the numbers on the wall. "In all our years, the *Wishes Made* and *Wishes Granted* counters have always matched…until now!"

"Momma, you need to calm down," Santa said. "We'll make this right."

"And how are we supposed to do that, Poppa?" she said, placing her hands on her hips. "You know the rules. She's too old now."

3

Stroking his beard, Santa read the letter again, and tilting his head, he touched the side of his nose with his finger as he paused to think about his options. Looking up, he said, "Percy, go see if you can get Him on the phone for me, will you please?"

The bells on the end of Percy's green stocking cap began to jingle, and the ones on the tips of his turned-up red shoes followed suit as the little man's knees started to shake. Wide-eyed, he squeaked, "Him, sir?"

"That's right."

"You…you…you mean *the* Him, sir?"

"Yes, Percy, that's exactly who I mean. Now, please, go do as I ask."

Swallowing hard, Percy took a deep breath and nodded his head. "Yes, sir," he said, quickly jingle-jangling out of the room.

"What are you planning to do?" Mrs. Claus asked.

Glancing at the letter, Santa said, "I'm going to ask him to relax the rules a bit."

"Oh, Poppa, I know you mean well, but after children stop believing in you, they're in His hands. You know that. And even if He said we could grant her wish, I'm afraid that what she's asking for we don't have in any of our workshops. A teddy bear would have worked when she was a child, but she's a grown woman now."

Hearing the tinkle of the bells announcing Percy's return, Santa turned his attention to the very nervous looking elf as he approached.

Holding the latest in mobile phones hard against his chest, Percy said, "Sir…um…He's…He's on the phone, but I…I couldn't put Him on hold. It…it…it just didn't seem right."

Smiling, Santa took the smartphone from his hand. "Thank you, Percy. Why don't you go back to your work, and we'll talk about sack linings later. Okay?"

"Yes, sir."

Watching as the elf shuffled out of the room, Santa took a deep breath before putting the phone to his ear.

For the next several minutes, Mrs. Claus sat silently as her husband pleaded his case to the man on the other end of the line.

Watching as her husband flicked off the phone, Mrs. Claus sat up straight. "Well?"

"We're in luck."

"He's going to allow it?"

"Yes and no."

Noticing the twinkle in her husband's eyes, Mrs. Claus crossed her arms, leaned back in her chair, and asked with a wary smile, "What exactly are you boys up to?"

Letting out a chuckle, Santa winked at his wife. "You know me too well."

"Yes, well centuries of living with you will do that," she said. "Now, come on…out with it."

Before Santa could answer, his administrative assistant, Lucy Bouncy-Bits, came flouncing into the room.

"An email for you, sir," she said politely, handing Santa a piece of paper.

"Thank you, Lucy. Do me a favor and find Percy for me. He should be in the stables."

"My pleasure, sir," she replied, flashing him a toothy smile before sauntering down the hall.

"So what's that?" Mrs. Claus asked, trying to see what was written on the paper in her husband's hand. Noticing that he didn't appear to hear what she had asked, she rolled her eyes remembering that Santa was as guilty of selective hearing as the rest of the world. Deciding to give him another minute, she waited patiently, but just as she was about to repeat her question, Percy dashed into the room.

Once again, out of breath and nervous, Percy slid to a stop next to Santa and all but shouted in the man's ear, "*Lucy said you wanted to see me, sir?*"

Chuckling at the little man's angst, Santa looked down and said, "Percy, relax. We all make mistakes, and accidents are bound to happen. The secret is to learn from them."

"Yes, sir."

"Now, I need you to visit our botanical workshop and bring me back some mistletoe."

"Mistletoe, sir?"

"Yes, Percy…three sprigs, please."

"Of mistletoe?"

Looking over the top of his reading glasses, Santa said, "Percy, I don't think that this young lady should have to wait any longer for her wish, but if you keep asking me to repeat myself, that's exactly what's going to happen. Now, since you're my lead elf, I was hoping that I could depend on you to help me correct this mistake, but if you feel the task too daunting for you to undertake…"

Percy's eyes flew open. "What? Absolutely not, sir," he said, snapping to attention. Saluting Kris Kringle, Percy said, "I'm your elf, sir! No job's too small or too large for Percy Giggly-Legs! I'll be back in a flash with your mistletoe, sir. Quicker than a flash…quicker than…than…than Rudolph, sir!"

Laughing as he watched the little, red-headed man sprint from the room, Santa turned his attention back to his wife and was met by a very curious look.

"Mistletoe? That's the best you could come up with?" she said, crossing her arms.

"Actually, it was His idea," Santa said. "While we were talking, He let it slip that she'll be attending three Christmas parties in the coming weeks, and He suggested that perhaps if we give her a nudge in the right direction, she might very well get her wish."

Tilting her head to the side, Mrs. Claus said, "A nudge? By using mistletoe?"

"It worked for us, didn't it?" Santa said, looking over the top of his reading glasses.

Mrs. Claus' cheeks darkened ever so slightly, and nodding her head, she asked, "So what's in the email?"

"Oh, it's just the addresses for the homes where the parties will be held," Santa said. Getting to his feet, he handed her the child's letter. "Do me a favor, hold on to this so we don't lose it again, and when Percy returns, send him to my office."

Grinning as he kissed her on the cheek, Mrs. Claus watched as Santa strode from the room. Looking at the folded piece of paper in her hand, she opened it and re-read the words of a four-year-old girl, which had been written some thirty years before.

Dear Mr. Santa,

My name is Diana, and I want a soul mate just like my Mommy and Daddy were before they had to go live with God. Aunt B says that's 'cos they loved each other so much. Because Mommy and Daddy are gone, my Aunt Brenda is drawing my words 'cos I'm only four and can't do words yet. I can do a D and an I and an A and an N and another A though. That says Diana.

I know I have to ask for a toy when I see Santa at the mall, but I miss my Mommy and Daddy, and I want to be like them. So I don't want a toy, I want a soul mate for Christmas. Someone to love me and so I don't have to be by myself anymore. Aunt Brenda says she's always going to be here for me, but I want the kind of lovey stuff like Mom and Dad had, with kisses and cuddles. Aunt Brenda is nice, but she is old, and smells funny. Can I have a prince like from my stories? They seem nice and have a horse.

Aunt Brenda says that she is drawing down what I'm saying, but she has something in her eye, so I have to go now. She's a good girl, most of the time. Can you get her a soul mate, too? For when I grow up and go to live in my fairy castle?

Hope the elves do all their jobs right and that Rudolph's nose glows properly.

D I A N A

***

"Why am I doing this again?" Diana Clarke asked, stepping into her high-heeled pumps.

"Because you're my best friend, and I need a date."

"You're not my type," Diana said, flashing a quick smile.

"Let me rephrase," Gwen Fowler said. "I need protection from Phelan."

Shaking her head, Diana said, "I have no idea why you still work for that man."

"I work for the firm. He's just head of the division where I'm assigned."

"By what you've told me, it sounds like he's more the tail end," Diana said, walking out of the bedroom.

"You'll get no argument there," Gwen said, following Diana down the stairs. "But since I'm a junior partner, I'm required to attend these parties, and you agreed to be my chaperone. Remember?"

"I agreed to go with you tonight, but I'm not sure about the other two."

"Why?"

Searching the hall closet for her coat, Diana said, "Gwen, Christmas is three weeks away. I can't spend every Saturday attending your office parties. I have things to do."

"Such as?"

With one arm in the sleeve of her coat, Diana stopped and stared at her friend in disbelief. Even for Gwen, that was a low blow. "Tell me again why you're my best friend?"

"That's not what I meant, and you know it," Gwen said, waving her hand through the air to dismiss Diana's interpretation. "You, yourself, said that you're not going to start looking for a new job until after the first, and this will cheer you up."

"And how do you figure that?"

"Well, for one thing, I'm sure there'll be some eligible bachelors there."

"Not interested," Diana said, grabbing her small clutch bag. "I think I've had enough disastrous relationships for one year, don't you?"

"You've only had three."

"Two," Diana said. Stopping to mentally tally her failed affairs, her shoulders slumped. "Shit, it was three, wasn't it?"

"Yes, but who's counting?"

"Apparently, you are," Diana said with a snort. "But no matter, because three's the charm, as they say, and I've had all the charm that one girl can handle this year." Seeing the taxi pull into her driveway, Diana asked, "You ready?"

"Yeah, let's go."

***

A few minutes later, settled in the back of the cab, Diana asked, "So, you never said...why the three separate parties this year?"

"After last year's fiasco, the partners all decided that it would be best to keep their clientele separated."

Pausing for a moment, Diana thought back to the previous year. Chuckling as she remembered the story Gwen had told her, she said, "Oh, I forgot about that."

"Yes, well, the firm lost a few clients shortly afterward, so Willoughby came up with the idea of having separate parties. Personally, I think she was just trying to save money."

"What do you mean? I would think three parties would be a hell of a lot more expensive than one."

"You're absolutely right, but since each gathering is catering to a specific division—"

"Oh, let me guess. The partners each pay for their own party."

"Yep, and trust me, that little detail has Lillian Willoughby's name written all over it. Frugal old biddy."

With a snigger, Diana said, "You're making her sound positively lovely."

Rolling her eyes, Gwen snickered. "She's hardly lovely, trust me, but it's probably the reason she's such a good divorce lawyer."

"How so?"

"Mrs. Willoughby looks like she could be anyone's mother, but behind that chubby-cheeked smile and those fluttering eyelashes of hers, is a pit bull waiting to rip the arms and legs off of some unsuspecting, soon-to-be, ex-wife."

"Wait. She only represents the husbands?"

Nodding her head, Gwen said, "She's as old school as you can get. I've been told that she absolutely adored her father. Quite the daddy's girl apparently, so in her eyes, all men are perfect. If a marriage goes south, it's because the woman wasn't doing her job."

"That's ridiculous!"

"That's Lillian Willoughby," Gwen said with a laugh. "To say the least, she's a piece of work."

"Well, then I'm glad I chose this party to attend, instead of hers."

"You're not that lucky."

"Huh?"

"She'll be there tonight."

"But this is Phelan's party."

"Yes, but all the partners have to attend each other's party, so they can represent the firm as a whole. It was part of the deal."

"Oh, so I'll meet all three?"

"Well, you'll definitely meet Ted Phelan."

"Is he really as bad as you make him out to be?"

"He's worse," Gwen said with a sigh as she leaned back in the seat. "He's a braggart who thinks he's got the answer to every woman's problem in his trousers. And when he sees you, Willoughby will be the least of *your* worries."

"Gwen!"

"Don't worry. I won't leave you alone with him, at least not for too long."

"What do you mean...not for too long? You better not leave me alone with him for a second!"

"I'm going to have to mingle."

"Then I'll mingle with you," Diana said, crossing her arms. "The last thing I need is some egotistical lawyer trying to get me into his bed!"

***

Entering the home of Theodore Phelan, Diana was helped out of her coat by a butler standing at the ready near the front door. Waiting for Gwen to do the same, Diana straightened her black jersey knit dress and took a few moments to look around the entrance hall. Seeing open-mouthed mementos of hunting trips hanging on almost every wall, and several golf trophies proudly displayed on nearby tables, Diana was fairly certain that Theodore Phelan was a bachelor, and absolutely positive that he was proud of it.

"Come on," Gwen said, gesturing toward a large archway. "That's the living room. I'm sure we'll find something to drink in there."

"Works for me," Diana said with a grin. Her high-heels clicking across the parquet floor, she followed Gwen to the doorway and peered inside. Diana wasn't impressed.

Rustic and manly, the khaki walls were accented by thick, walnut-stained moldings, and huge ebony timbers ran across the ceiling, casting an oppressive darkness over the spacious room. Area rugs with hunting motifs covered the floor, and the two patio doors on the far wall were framed in drapes the color of mud. If it wasn't for the narrow, artificial Christmas tree in the corner of the room, decorated with one strand of multi-colored lights thrown haphazardly over its branches, the décor could have been easily described with just one word. Brown.

Mentally shaking her head, Diana walked inside and immediately wished that she hadn't. Cigar smoke hung in the air, and mixed with the pungent smell of an overabundance of perfume and cologne, her eyes immediately began to water. Blinking a few times to clear the sting, she was finally able to scan the room. Having paid more attention to her surroundings than to the men and women milling about, it quickly became apparent why Gwen had preferred not to come alone. Although Diana was fairly certain that she had never personally met any of those in attendance, she knew who they were. She read the newspaper, and she watched the news.

Theodore Phelan's expertise was criminal law, but his clients weren't just any criminals. Hiding behind their three-piece suits, chains of gold and rings encrusted with diamonds, these were the men who made their living off of other people's pain. Their millions had been earned by the promises of protection offered to those less fortunate, and by the illegal drugs their workforce sold in alleyways and office buildings. Women walking the street in stilettos and miniskirts also contributed to their fund, as well as politicians needing a bit of help in swaying their constituents' votes. These were the men who ruled the underworld, and by the looks of some of the women accompanying them, Diana couldn't help but wonder if a few of the ladies hadn't made their home on street corners at one time in their lives.

In sequined dresses plunging low in the front and high in the hem, the women who had their arms hooked through those belonging to Phelan's clientele had been nipped and tucked to perfection. Their over-amplified bosoms strained against the glittery fabric holding them captive, and their makeup had been applied in a thickness equaling grout. Sipping their champagne from hollow-stemmed glasses, they giggled and tickled their way through conversations they didn't understand, but no one seemed to care. The only knowledge they were required to share would come later in the night…and it would be carnal.

With the room overflowing with people, Diana glanced back at Gwen for directions to the bar, but when she saw the false smile painted on her friend's face, Diana slowly turned around. Confidently striding toward her was a tall, broad-shouldered man with graying brown hair and dark, piercing eyes that seemed to be locked on Diana as if she was a beacon in the night.

He had noticed her as soon as she walked into the room. With the help of three-inch high heels, her calves were stretched and shapely, and her dark-brown hair, worn loose and flowing, shimmered in the light. Compared to the other women attending his party, her garb was plain, but the more he ogled, the more his mouth watered, and the more he realized that she didn't need silks, satins and rhinestones to get attention. She did it in a simple black dress that hugged every curve she owned.

"Now, who do we have here?" Ted Phelan said, leering at Diana.

"Mr. Phelan," Gwen began, motioning to Diana. "This is my friend, Diana Clarke. Since Adam's out of—"

Brushing off Gwen's statement with a shake of his head, he extended his hand to Diana. "Ted Phelan. Pleasure to meet you, Diana."

"Thank you," Diana said, taking his hand. Trying not to blanch at the damp palm pressed against hers, she smiled back, and as soon as he let go of her hand, Diana straightened her dress in an attempt to wipe off the sweat. Watching as he tried his best to undress her with his eyes, Diana fought the urge to scold the man for his rudeness. However, remembering that he was Gwen's boss, she bit her lip and forced herself to smile.

"I must say, that dress does things to me. If you know what I mean," Ted said with a wink.

Raising her chin, Diana looked him in the eye. Debating for only a moment, she replied, "I'm afraid they probably wouldn't have it in your size, Ted, but I'll be more than happy to give you the name of the shop where I bought it, if you'd like."

Narrowing his eyes, he quickly glanced in Gwen's direction and then back at Diana. "You're a feisty one, I'll give you that," he said with a smarmy leer. "But I'm a man who loves the challenge of the hunt."

Without missing a beat, Diana said, "Yes, I noticed all those poor dead animals hanging on your walls. Did you chase them down and kill them with your bare hands?"

Straightening his shoulders, Phelan looked around the room. Refusing to allow his agitation to show, he returned his gaze to Diana, and then again, blatantly allowed his eyes to take in her view. His annoyance growing when she didn't blink an eye at his perusal, he decided to cut his losses. "Perhaps later, you and I can talk more, but right now I need to go take care of my guests. I'm sure you understand."

"Of course. Please don't let me keep you," Diana said, displaying a half-hearted smile.

Without saying another word, Phelan walked away, and immediately Diana turned to Gwen and said, "I'm sorry."

"About what?"

"He's your boss."

"True, but he's also an ass, and by the end of the night, he'll have enough scotch in him to sink a ship. Trust me, Diana, he won't remember a thing. Now, let's go get a drink."

CHAPTER TWO

A little man wearing a floppy, pointed cap and dressed in an outfit of red and green pranced into the house unnoticed. He smelled of peppermint and sugar cookies, and the bells on his clothes jingled with every step he took, but those around him were completely ignorant of his existence. Even though he had the ability to become visible to the men, women and children who lived outside of Santa's village if he so desired, tonight his mission was stealth.

Being slightly shorter than a yardstick, on his back, he carried a small sack filled with the essentials of someone vertically challenged. After weaving his way through the legs of the people who filled the room, he reached the fireplace and opened his backpack. Taking out a magic ladder, he extended it to the mantle and quickly scampered up the rungs. Perched on the shelf, he pulled a small photograph from his pocket and looked out over the room. His eyes darted from one woman to the next, and frowning that none matched the lady in the picture Santa had given him, he put it back in his pocket and sighed. Ever vigilant, he remained sitting cross-legged on the shelf until he finally saw her walk into the room. He smiled. She was pretty.

His intention had been to stay on the mantle until it was time for her to leave, but the cigar smoke in the air had risen around him, encasing him in a smelly, hazy cloud. Noticing that Diana had taken a seat in the far corner of the room to enjoy some appetizers, he leapt at the chance to get away from the second-hand smoke for a few minutes. Sliding down the ladder, he took a deep breath of the slightly fresher air. Catching a whiff of the hors d'oeuvres being served, his stomach began to grumble, and nimbly scurrying through the crowd, he stepped up to the table of food and quickly perused the selection. Curling his lip at the sight of the vegetable tray, he ate a few bits of cheese from a platter before dipping some chips into a taco dip. Shrugging his shoulders at the remaining selection, he stuffed a few bread rolls in his pocket, and was about return to his lookout point when he felt something being poured over his head. Jumping back from the table, Percy looked up to see the host of the party weaving above him with an empty glass in his hand. Taking a sniff of the liquid covering his outfit, Percy smiled. Scotch.

Even though he knew he wasn't supposed to drink on duty, Percy was an adult, albeit a very small one, and he was thirsty. Deciding that a few sips wouldn't hurt, he picked up an empty glass, rung out his cap and returned to the fireplace mantle with the dregs in hand. It wasn't much, but it was, after all, scotch. Sipping the liquor, he snacked on the dinner rolls and watched as the evening progressed, patiently waiting to complete his task.

***

Finding Diana hiding out near the table filled with finger-foods on silver trays, Gwen asked, "Where's your drink?"

"I decided that I'd best stay sober," Diana answered, her eyes darting around the room.

"Why? I can't get drunk because technically, I'm working, but there's no reason why you can't have some fun."

"Gwen, in the past two hours, I've been called honey, darling, sweetheart, cutesy, *and* little lady. Six men have asked for my phone number. Two tried to get me to go upstairs, and one patted me on my ass!"

"Sorry, but now you know why Adam didn't want me to come alone," Gwen said with a snicker.

"Well, at least you're married! I feel like any minute I'm going to be put up for auction!"

Giggling, Gwen gave Diana a hug. "I'm sorry. I guess I owe you one – huh?"

"Yes, you do, so how about paying up now, and let's get out of here."

"Oh, I wish I could, but I have a few more meet-and-greets to do. I'm sorry."

Letting out an exasperated sigh, Diana was about to plead her case when a loud, cackling laugh overwhelmed the room. Flinching at the noise, she looked over her shoulder and saw a dumpy woman wearing an overly tight, green satin dress.

"Let me guess, Lillian Willoughby?" Diana said quietly.

"How could you tell?" Gwen answered with a grin. "Would you like me to introduce you?"

Playfully shuddering, Diana said, "Not if you value our friendship." Returning her attention to the bar area for a second, she asked, "So, who's the other woman?"

"Which one?"

"The blonde by the bar."

Looking in that direction, Gwen smiled. "Oh, that's the other partner, Jamison Nash."

For the past hour, Diana had been intrigued by the woman. She seemed an anomaly in a room filled with pomp. Dressed in a gray, double-breasted tailored suit, she had an aura of elegant simplicity about her. There was no man on her arm, nor did she appear to need one, and although she was surrounded by bling, she didn't seem to notice. Apparently more at ease chatting with the bartender than mingling among the guests, she stood sipping her wine, occasionally glancing at her watch as the evening slowly moved along.

Diana's eyes gradually found their way back to Jamison Nash. Scrutinizing for a moment, she turned and looked at Gwen. "So, what's wrong with her?"

"What do you mean?"

"Well, Phelan is a lecher of gargantuan proportions, and Willoughby is...well, Willoughby, and since Nash has been sitting over there by herself for almost an hour, I just assumed she had issues, too."

"The only issue Jamie Nash has is that she's as honest as the day is long, and she'll give you the shirt off her back if you need it."

"Then how did she end up with Phelan and Willoughby?"

"The firm was started by their grandfathers, and in Jamie's case, her father. They all inherited their shares of the business from them."

"Oh."

"There's a rumor going around that she wants to leave the firm, but I doubt that it's true. It's one of the best in New York, and with the income the three divisions generate, it helps pay for all her pro bono work. Personally, I think Willoughby just started it in hopes of grabbing up some of Jamie's paralegals."

"Pro bono?"

"Yeah, it means—"

"Gwen, I know what it means."

"Oh, right," Gwen said with a guilty smile. "Anyway, Jamie has a lot of causes, and when she's not dealing with the corporate law side of things, she spends her time righting the wrongs of those less fortunate."

"Sounds admirable."

"It is. It's actually the reason I wanted to work for Phelan, Willoughby and Nash. I'd love to work in her division, but since she's the nicest of the three partners, the jobs aren't readily available."

"I can imagine."

Noticing Phelan waving for her to join him, Gwen said, "Ted's calling me again. You going to be okay?"

"Yeah, I'll be fine. I think maybe I'll go outside and get some fresh air."

"Okay. I'll be back as soon as I can," Gwen said, giving Diana a quick smile before she headed in Phelan's direction.

Seeing a clearing in the crowd, Diana made her way to the patio doors, and quietly slipped outside. Filling her lungs with clean, crisp winter air, she walked over to the iron railing surrounding the porch, and taking another deep breath, she looked up and smiled at the sight of the blue-black sky, dotted by hundreds of stars. A slight breeze caused a shiver to run down her spine, and briskly rubbing her arms, Diana was about to go back inside when she felt something being draped over her shoulders.

"What the fu—" Diana said, whipping around. Assuming that it was Phelan or one of his over-stuffed clients, when she came face-to-face with Jamison Nash, she stopped her sentence just short of embarrassing.

"Oh, sorry," Diana said, offering the woman an apologetic smile. "I thought you were Mr. Phelan."

"Well, in that case, I should consider myself lucky that I didn't get slapped in the face," the woman said with a chuckle, extending her hand. "I'm Jamie Nash."

"Diana Clarke," Diana said, returning the gesture. Impressed by the mixture of strength and softness in the woman's grip, the slightest hint of sadness washed over Diana when their hands finally parted.

"I'm sorry if I frightened you," Jamie said, cupping her hands against the breeze to light her cigarette. "But you looked like you were cold."

Diana's eyes flew open. Realizing that she was still wearing Jamie's suit jacket, she took it off and held it out. "Oh, here, this is yours."

Shaking her head, Jaime took the coat and again, draped it over Diana's shoulders. "I'm fine. You're the one that's shivering."

Although Diana welcomed the warmth of the satin-lined, worsted wool jacket, as she pulled it closer around her body, she half-heartedly tried one more time. "Are you sure?"

"Consider it my attempt at chivalry," Jamie said with a wink.

"They say it's dead…chivalry, I mean."

"Well, there you go then. Because of you, it's risen from the grave and will live for yet another day."

Noticing the sleeves of Jamie's crisp, white silk shirt billowing in the breeze, Diana snickered. "Yes, but will you? It's freezing out here."

Taking another drag of her cigarette, Jamie hunched her shoulders against the cold. "I'll survive long enough to finish this."

"Isn't that a contradiction in terms?"

With a snort, Jamie nodded her head. "Touché." Debating on how to keep the conversation going, Jamie's thoughts were interrupted when a strong gust of frigid wind whipped across the patio, its iciness slicing through her blouse in an instant. Turning her back against the force of it, she blurted, "Holy Mother of God!"

Trying to hold back her giggle, Diana said, "You okay?"

"Yes, but I think chivalry just died again. Do you mind if we go back inside?"

"I thought you'd never ask," Diana said, flashing a quick grin as she headed for the door, but before she could reach for the knob, Jamie was there to open it.

"Allow me."

"I thought chivalry just died?"

"It did, but you're moving too slow."

Once inside, Diana returned the jacket to its owner, and as Jamie slipped it on, she asked, "Can I buy you a drink?"

"I thought they were free," Diana said with a twinkle in her eye.

With a laugh, Jamie tried again. "Can I *get* you a drink?"

Finding herself enjoying the woman's company, Diana said softly, "Yes, please."

Managing to get through the throng of people standing in the middle of the room, as they reached the bar, Jamie asked, "What would you like?"

"Red wine, I think."

Turning to the bartender, Jamie said, "Tony, two glasses of my wine, please."

"*Your* wine?" Diana asked.

"I'm afraid that Phelan's taste in wine matches his taste in decorating. I always bring a bottle," Jamie said, handing Diana a glass. "I hope you like Syrah. It can be rather intense if you're not used to it."

Intrigued by Jamie's description, Diana's eyes never left Jamie's as she brought the glass to her lips. Inhaling the bouquet of blackberry and cloves, she took a sip and smiled as her palate was pleasured by not only the flavors of the aroma, but also a hint of licorice and black currant.

"It's marvelous," Diana said, taking another sip.

A radiant smile graced Jamie's face. "I'm glad you like it," she said softly, gesturing toward two empty barstools. "Shall we?"

For the first time since she had walked into Ted Phelan's house, Diana felt at ease. No longer concerned with the men leering at her, or the sound of Willoughby cackling somewhere in the room, Diana's attention was focused on only one thing. Jamie Nash.

Unlike the rich and infamous milling about the room, and the pompous host who could be heard over the rest, crowing about his latest kill, Jamie seemed to be much like the wine she drank. Intense, but with just enough spice to make her interesting, and a teasing finish that kept you coming back for more…and Diana wanted more. Jamie's air of charismatic confidence was refreshing. Captivated by her easy-going nature, Diana found herself looking forward to spending the rest of the evening sipping wine and chatting with the lawyer who was wearing an Italian suit tailored to absolute perfection. Diana wanted to know the significance of the small signet ring Jamie wore on her pinky, and the name of the unbelievably provocative cologne she was wearing. As Diana was unconsciously breathing deep the fragrance, there was one more thing she noticed. Jamie Nash was gorgeous.

Tall and slender, with short golden-blonde hair and eyes the color of sapphires, Jamie's beauty was flawless. In direct contrast to the buxom brunettes and bouffant redheads roaming the room wearing obnoxiously large jewels on their fingers, wrists and necks, Jamie didn't seem to need any enhancement to be beautiful. She just was.

Lost in her thoughts, Diana took a sip of wine. Totally unaware that she had just spent the last few minutes perusing Jamison Nash from head to toe, when she raised her eyes again and found Jamie smiling back at her, Diana's cheeks flamed instantly.

Laughing at the sight of the woman's blush, Jamie asked, "You always stare like that?"

"Actually, I don't, but I was trying to figure out how a person like you could ever work with Ted Phelan."

"A person like me?"

"Well, it's obvious that Phelan considers himself a ladies' man and looking the way you do—"

The words died in Diana's throat when a devastating smile instantly appeared on Jamie's face, and as if that wasn't enough, when Jamie added a raised eyebrow and a slight tilt of her head, Diana's entire body tingled. The look was playful, but it was also sexy. It was beyond sexy.

Praying that her cheeks weren't the color of the wine in her glass, Diana decided the only course of action was nonchalance…and more wine. After taking a healthy swallow of the Syrah, she simply said, "What I mean is, I would think that you'd be fighting him off every day. That's all."

"Thanks for the compliment, but you've got a few things wrong," Jamie said, softening her smile.

"Such as?"

"Well, first, I don't work with Phelan. He handles criminal law, and I handle corporate."

"Aren't they the same thing?"

With a grin, Jamie replied, "I suppose at times they can be, but my specialty is contracts and his is… well, his is keeping criminals out of jail."

"Why would he want to do that?"

"Because there are a lot of people who will pay a lot of money not to go to prison, and even though Phelan can be an ass at times, he knows the law like the back of his hand. He knows where all the loopholes are, and he's a master at knowing precedents *and* setting them. And he can cast such a large shadow of doubt over evidence presented, that even the criminal starts believing that they didn't commit the crime."

"You sound like you respect him."

Pausing for a moment, Jamie said, "I respect the man's knowledge, but not the man, if that makes sense."

"Does he respect you?"

"No," Jamie said with a snort.

"Why not?"

"Because Phelan's work takes him down into the trenches, and mine takes me to elevators leading to the fortieth floor."

"Oh, I see," Diana said, taking a sip of wine. "But Gwen said you do a lot of pro bono work."

MISTLETOE

Hearing the familiar name, Jamie blanched. "Oh, Christ, please tell me you're not one of Phelan's clients."

"What? Why would you think that?"

"You just mentioned Gwen, and I'm assuming you mean Gwen Fowler."

"I do."

"She works in Ted's division."

"And she's also my best friend. Her husband is out of town, so she asked me to be her escort tonight."

"Oh, thank God," Jamie said, emptying what was left in her glass in one swallow. "That's why I hate coming to these things. You never know who you're talking to, and you can easily wind up putting your foot in your mouth."

"Is that something you do often?"

"What's that?"

"Put your foot in your mouth?"

"No, it only seems to happen when I find myself in the company of a beautiful woman."

While she was in no way offended by the words Jamie had spoken, Diana found herself struggling to respond. Having a hard time wrapping her head around the fact that she took pleasure knowing Jamie found her attractive, Diana's confusion showed in her expression.

Misreading the look on Diana's face, Jamie quickly said, "I'm sorry, I shouldn't have said that."

33

A strange feeling washed over Diana, and although she was confused by it, the wine had warmed her blood enough to lower her inhibitions just a tad. Raising her eyes to meet Jamie's, in the sexiest voice she could produce, Diana asked, "Why, don't you think I'm beautiful?"

It was all Jamie could do not grunt out loud at the feeling of her libido coming to life between her legs.

Her attendance had been mandatory. Arriving on time, she had been met by Phelan at the door and then allowed herself to be led around the room, shaking the hands of men she loathed. It was an act, and both Phelan and she knew it, but it was required, and in a few weeks, he would return the favor. Such was their relationship. It was a co-existence necessary in order to keep their firm on the top ten list, and while there was no love lost between them, neither would allow their disdain for each other to damage the company their families had started decades before.

Deciding that three hours would be enough time to fulfill her obligation to Phelan, Willoughby and Nash, Jamie staked her claim at the end of the bar and waited patiently for the clock to strike ten. Rarely looking up from her wine glass, she didn't notice Diana Clarke until she walked outside for a smoke. Somewhat surprised to see a woman in attendance wearing a simple black knit dress, rather than something glitzy and two sizes too small, when she noticed Diana shivering in the cold night air, Jamie didn't think twice before lending the woman her jacket. She had no ulterior motive, and no strings were attached to the comfort that she offered. It was a simple gesture of friendship to a faceless stranger in need. It was, in fact, the essence of Jamie Nash, but when Diana turned around and Jamie found herself looking at the most beautiful woman she had ever seen in her life, her plan to leave the party precisely at ten went straight out the window.

Taking a sip of wine, Jamie mentally scolded her lower half for not behaving itself. Up until that moment, the mood had been playful and friendly, and Jamie didn't want it to change. Sensing just a hint of whimsy in Diana's provocative tone, Jamie lowered her eyes and allowed them to travel slowly up Diana's body. When her eyes met Diana's, Jamie said, "You'll do, I suppose."

Tossing back her head, Diana burst out laughing, and the sound of her mirth brought yet another smile to Jamie's face.

"Well, it sounds like you're having fun," Gwen said as she emerged from the crowd. "Good evening, Miss Nash."

Shaking her head, Jamie said, "Gwen, I've told you a dozen times to call me Jamie. Now please, drop the formalities."

Offering an apologetic smile in Jamie's direction, Gwen touched Diana on the sleeve. "Phelan is on his way to one hell of a hangover, so we can leave now. He won't miss me, and even if he does, he won't remember it in the morning."

"Oh," Diana said. "Um…okay."

"I'm just going to use the bathroom. Meet you out front, all right?"

"Yeah, yeah…I'll be there in a minute."

"Good night, Miss…erm…Jamie."

"Good night, Gwen, and please drive safe," Jamie said. Watching as Gwen headed for the door, Jamie turned her attention back to Diana. "Well, it seems I need to wish you a good night also."

"I'm sorry," Diana said. "I was hoping we'd have more time to talk."

"So was I," Jamie said softly.

"Um…well, I'd best go find Gwen," Diana said, finishing the wine in her glass. "Thank you for the wine and the use of your jacket."

Although tempted to offer Diana a ride home, Jamie didn't want to assume anything. A lighthearted chat was one thing, but presuming that the woman wanted anything more than just friendly conversation, was quite another. Not allowing her disappointment to creep into the tone of her voice, Jamie said lightly, "It was my pleasure."

Flashing Jamie a toothy grin, Diana turned to walk away, but when she felt Jamie's hand on her arm, she stopped dead in her tracks. Swallowing hard at the feeling of butterflies fluttering in her stomach, Diana turned back around.

"I was wondering, if...if you might be escorting Gwen to Lillian's party next week?" Jamie asked.

"To tell you the truth, I wasn't planning on it, but I think I've changed my mind."

"Can I ask why?"

"Do you really need to?" Diana said. Not waiting for Jamie to answer, Diana flashed another quick smile before making her way through the crowd. When she finally reached the large archway which led back to the entrance hall, Diana was greeted by a very smug and a very drunk Theodore Phelan.

"Not so fast," he said with a sneer, holding out his arm to block her escape. "You're not going anywhere, yet."

Forced to come to an abrupt halt, Diana said, "Pardon me?"

"You owe me a kiss," Phelan said, looking down his nose at her.

Taking a step back, Diana stiffened. "Excuse me?"

Pointing above her head, he said, "I don't know who put it there, but since they did, I intend to take full advantage of it."

Looking up, when Diana saw the sprig of mistletoe, she paled. Trying to think of something to say, she paused for a second, and then a familiar voice rang out.

"In your dreams, Phelan," Jamie said, striding to the doorway. "Now let her pass."

Keeping his voice low so that others wouldn't hear, Phelan leaned in and said, "This is my house, Nash, not yours. And since this is *my* Christmas party and that goddamn weed is hanging over *my* doorway, tradition dictates that this lovely lady doesn't leave until she gets kissed."

Jamie watched as Phelan looked back at Diana, hungrily licking his lips in anticipation, but before he could make his move, Jamie made hers.

Reaching over, she slipped her hand behind Diana's neck and pulled her close. Jamie's intention was only to satisfy tradition with a mere brush of her lips, but once they touched Diana's, tradition was quickly forgotten.

It happened so fast that by the time Diana realized that Jamie was about to kiss her, their lips were already touching. The scent of the cologne which Diana had admired from afar now filled her nostrils, and spellbound, Diana closed her eyes and allowed the kiss to continue.

Jamie was in trouble. There was no doubt about it. The kiss should have only lasted for a second, or maybe two, but they were well past five and rapidly heading toward ten or twenty. Jamie knew that she should pull away. She was stepping way over the line with a woman she had just met, but oh, what a woman. Diana's lips were the softest that Jamie had ever touched, and her flavor was more intoxicating than the finest of wines. For a few seconds more, Jamie allowed herself to get lost in the heady rush of their first kiss.

With a heavy heart, Jamie finally pulled away, and as Diana opened her eyes, Jamie looked over at Phelan. "Consider her kissed. Now, let her pass."

Slack-jawed, Phelan backed away from the door, and without saying a word, Diana walked out.

***

As a fire danced in the hearth, Santa sat behind his desk, sipping hot chocolate. Taking another letter from the pile stacked to his right, he smiled as he read what was written. Checking the list displayed on his computer, he made yet another notation in the *Nice* column and then entered the child's wish. Placing the note aside, he picked up the next, but stopped when he heard the tinkling of bells. Looking up, he grinned when he saw Percy Giggly-Legs appear in the doorway.

"There you are. It was getting a bit late. I was starting to worry," Santa said.

"It took longer than expected, sir," Percy said, shuffling over to the desk.

Catching a whiff of his lead elf, Santa's eyes flew open. "Percy! You smell like you spent the night in a distillery."

"Oh, yes, sir...I mean...I mean, no sir. Mr. Phelan's house was filled with people drinking and smoking. I couldn't get away from it and still do my job."

"I see," Santa said, eyeing the elf. "And did you?"

"No, sir. Not a drop...well, maybe a splash, but it wasn't my fault. Honest."

Shaking his head, Santa looked over the top of his reading glasses. "Percy, I was talking about the mistletoe."

"Oh," Percy replied as a slight blush crossed his cheeks.

"So, tell me, how did it go?"

Hanging his head, Percy said, "I don't think it worked, sir."

"What do you mean? What happened?"

"Well, I did as you told me, and hung the mistletoe where Miss Diana would be sure to walk under it, but when Mr. Phelan tried to kiss her, she refused."

"Mr. Phelan?"

"Yes, sir. Mr. Theodore Phelan. He was the host of the party tonight."

Turning to his computer, Santa tapped away at the keys. Running a search in his *Naughty and Nice* database, his brow furrowed when he saw the amount of times that little Teddy Phelan had appeared on the *Naughty* side of the list. Looking over at the elf, Santa said, "Percy, I'm not sure Mr. Phelan was supposed to be the one who kissed Miss Diana tonight."

"No?"

"Definitely not," Santa said, shaking his head.

"I'm glad, sir."

"You are?"

"Yes, sir. I didn't like Mr. Phelan very much."

"By the sounds of it, neither did Miss Diana."

"No, sir. She was actually quite determined about not being kissed by him, sir."

"So, are you saying that no one kissed Miss Diana under our mistletoe?"

"Um…no, sir," Percy said quietly. Pulling a piece of paper from his pocket, he handed it to Santa. "The lady's name is Jamison Nash. I wrote it down so I wouldn't forget it."

"A lady?"

Blushing slightly, Percy nodded his head. "Yes, sir."

Placing his finger to the side of his nose, Santa thought for a moment before he said with a smile, "I see."

"Santa?"

Looking up from the paper in his hand, Santa said, "Yes, Percy."

"Does this mean that Miss Diana is like Humphrey Sweet-Cheeks and Egbert Jelly-Belly?"

With a chuckle, Santa nodded his head. "I think so, yes."

"I like Humphrey and Egbert, sir," Percy said, his entire face spreading into a smile.

"So do I."

CHAPTER THREE

Linda Burke flicked on the lights in the outer office as she strolled into the room. Noticing that light was streaming from under the door leading to Jamie's office, she glanced at the coffee pot and smiled. Setting down her handbag and coat, she turned on her computer, looked at the papers stacked on her desk, and then walked over to fill two mugs with coffee. Tapping lightly on Jamie's door, she opened it and walked inside.

Theirs was a unique relationship. It had begun with an impromptu game of hide-and-seek when a very impatient six-year-old was waiting for her father to get off the phone, and over the years, their friendship continued to grow. Having worked as Sebastian Nash's secretary for almost thirty years, Linda had been able to watch Jamie grow from a small knobby-kneed child into a woman, confident and beautiful. Linda had attended Jamie's birthday parties and her graduations, and the pride that filled Linda's chest when Jamie graduated from law school at the top of her class, equaled that of a parent.

When Sebastian decided to take an early retirement, and Jamie assumed his role as acting partner, her first priority was to offer Linda the role of her assistant, and Linda leapt at the chance. With years of history to draw upon, and a friendship that was strong and sound, they were two acting as one, and the envy of many who worked at Phelan, Willoughby and Nash.

"Good morning. How was your trip?" Linda chirped.

Looking up from her desk, Jamie smiled back. "It was long, but lucrative," she said, wiggling her eyebrows. "I put the contracts on your desk. You just need to make the corrections I noted in the margins, and then I'll initial them, and we can send them along."

"I already saw them, and you'll have them back within the hour," Linda said as she handed Jamie one of the mugs of coffee. Noticing that she was studying her appointment calendar for the month, Linda leaned over to take a look.

Accustomed to seeing every day filled up with meetings, conference calls and the like, when she saw that the next few weeks had almost nothing etched in stone, Linda said, "A bit sparse, isn't it?"

"It's that time of the year," Jamie said, leaning back in her chair. "And since I'm still trying to finalize some things for the party, a few lackluster weeks is just what this party planner needs."

"Why do I think you're looking forward to this?"

"Because I am," Jamie said with a wide smile. "I'm just hoping that Santa Claus is on my side."

"Don't you mean, Mother Nature?"

"Yeah, her, too."

Walking back toward her office, Linda turned and asked, "Oh, by the way, how was Phelan's party?"

"Let's see," Jamie said, pondering her wording. "It was filled with presumably innocent criminals and their not-so-presumably intelligent silicone-breasted floozies. Food was horrid, and Phelan got drunk."

"Oh dear, he didn't cause a scene, did he?"

"Nothing I couldn't handle," Jamie replied. As soon as the words left her mouth, Jamie's thoughts returned to a woman who had spent the better part of the last four days taking up residence in Jamie's dreams. A woman with brown eyes and hair the color of espresso, who, when she smiled, displayed the most adorable dimples Jamie had ever seen. A woman who Jamie *did* want to handle in ways that made her blush, but unfortunately, she was also a woman who probably never wanted to talk to Jamie again.

Diana had left Phelan's house without so much as a glance in Jamie's direction, and a few minutes later, Jamie followed suit. Driving home, she replayed the events of the evening in her mind, and acting as her own judge and jury, Jamie found herself guilty of utter stupidity. She acted without thinking. She kissed a woman she had only known for a few minutes. She royally fucked up. Guilty as charged.

Rubbing her neck to relieve the tension that was building, Jamie let out a sigh. All she wanted to do was go back in time and start again. She wanted to return to the friendly banter. She wanted the ease of casual without the weight of something more…but most of all, she wanted Diana Clarke.

"Jamie!"

Startled from her thoughts, Jamie looked up. "I'm sorry, Linda, what was that?"

"I asked if you needed anything else." Linda said, cocking her head to the side. "Are you okay?"

"What? Yes, I'm fine. Why?"

"You just seem a bit…um…distracted."

"Sorry. Just a few long days, that's all."

Glancing at the clock on the wall, Linda said, "Okay, well if you don't need me for anything, I'll go get those contracts sorted."

Standing at the door, Linda waited for a response, but when none was given, she simply shrugged her shoulders, walked out the door and quietly closed it behind her.

***

"I can't thank you enough for coming up."

"What do you mean?" Diana asked as her aunt came into the living room carrying two cups of tea. "I wouldn't have missed Joanie's baby shower for the world. It's been planned for weeks."

Sitting next to her niece, Brenda Clarke handed Diana one of the cups. "I know, but you'll be here for Christmas, and what with your situation, I wasn't sure that you could afford to make the trip twice."

Puzzled, Diana stared back at her aunt. "What in the world are you talking about? Flights from New York to Burlington are cheap enough."

"I just thought, since you don't have a job…"

Realizing what her aunt was worried about, Diana rolled her eyes. "Brenda, exactly how many piggy banks *did* I have as a child?"

"What?"

Laughing, Diana reached out and touched her aunt's knee. "I'm fine. I have plenty in savings to see me through. Honest."

Studying her niece, the woman asked, "Are you sure?"

"Yes!" Diana exclaimed with a laugh. "Trust me, I'm fine."

"Well then, what's been on your mind for these past two days? You've been preoccupied since you got here?"

"Have I?" Diana asked, taking a quick sip of tea.

"Oh, sweetheart, you know you have. You sit by the window most of the afternoon pretending to read, but instead, you spend the entire time staring off into space. You remind me of your father when he—" Brenda's mouth snapped shut as a memory came rushing back, and looking at her niece, Brenda's smile grew wide. Sitting up straight, she stated, "You're in love!"

Nearly dropping her cup of tea, Diana blurted, "Excuse me!"

"I said, you're in love."

"I am not!"

"Yes, you are."

"Oh, you're deranged," Diana muttered.

"Maybe so, but you're still in love."

"Will you *please* stop saying that?"

"Only when you stop denying it."

"I'm denying it because it isn't true," Diana said, getting to her feet. Grasping for straws, Diana said the first thing that came to mind. "You said it yourself, I'm unemployed and—"

"Oh, no you don't," Brenda said, waggling her finger. "You just told me that your finances would carry you through. And you and I both know that with your background, you won't have any problem finding another job, which leads me right back to the fact that you're in love."

"How can I convince you that I'm not?" Diana said, eyeing the woman who had raised her.

Thinking for a moment, Brenda asked, "Did I ever tell you about the first time your father met your mother?"

"What?"

"You heard me."

"Um…no, I don't think so, but you never talked about them that much. I wasn't sure if it was to ease my pain or yours."

"A little of both, I suspect," Brenda said quietly. "You were so young and so confused. It didn't make sense to dwell on the past and keep the wound open, so I didn't. I'm sorry."

"No worries," Diana said with a soft smile. "You always answered my questions when I asked about them, and besides, if I remember correctly, I was quite a handful back then."

"You most certainly were!" Brenda said with a snicker. "I'm glad you grew out of that when you hit your twenties."

"Hey!"

Both women began to laugh remembering their arguments over clothing, boyfriends and curfews. After a few minutes, Diana asked, "So what's a story about my parents got to do with me convincing you that I'm not in love?"

Patting the cushion next to her, Brenda said, "Come. Sit back down and I'll explain."

Returning to her spot on the sofa, Diana pursed her lips as she eyed her aunt suspiciously. "So, enlighten me."

Amused by her niece's defensiveness, Brenda said, "When your father was sixteen, your grandparents insisted that he go to the final school dance of the year. He was a very smart young man, and involved in every sport there was, but when it came to social gatherings, he avoided them like the plague."

"Why?"

"He was shy, and even though he was an extremely handsome, he felt totally uncomfortable around girls. He managed to come up with excuses for all the other school dances, but by the time the last one rolled around, he had run out, so reluctantly he went.

"I don't think I'll ever forget that night. Mom and Dad had gone to bed, but I had stayed up to read for a while. Ross walked in just after ten, and I swear, when he came through the door, it was as if someone had turned up the lights. His smile was so bright it was almost laughable."

"I'm not smiling like that," Diana stated.

"No, you're not, but there's more to this story, if you don't mind," Brenda said, her eyes sparkling with amusement.

Leaning back into the sofa, Diana crossed her arms and said, "Fine. I'm listening."

"Like I was saying, your father appeared to be in a very good mood when he came home that night, but after changing his clothes, he came back downstairs, sat down, picked up a magazine and proceeded to stare off into space for over an hour without saying a word. Of course, I was a bit confused because one minute he seemed happy and then the next…the next he seemed almost mystified. Beyond curious, I finally asked him what had happened at the dance, and he told me that he had met a girl. I think his exact words were…a wonderful, beautiful girl."

Goosebumps appeared on Diana's arms, and quietly she asked, "My mother?"

"Yes," Brenda said in a whisper, looking at her niece. "Oh, he must have rattled on for a good hour about Kathleen, telling me everything he could remember about this girl he had just met."

"Wait, it was a school dance. Wouldn't they have known each other already?"

"No, your mother had been visiting her cousin for the weekend, and apparently the girl's date became ill, so Kathleen agreed to go in his place. Safety in numbers, I suppose, but the point of my story is that the look on your father's face that night, when he *fell in love* with your mother, is the same look you've been wearing for the past two days."

"Oh," Diana said softly.

"Are you still going to deny it?"

Refusing to make eye contact, Diana played with a loose thread on her sweater for a few moments. Finally, with a shrug, she said, "Is there any point?"

Sensing that something was troubling her niece, Brenda asked, "Do you want to talk about it?"

"If you don't mind, I'd rather not. It's a bit confusing."

"I'm here to listen, and you never know, it could help."

Letting out a long breath, Diana said, "I don't even know this person. I mean, we met at a party last week and only talked for a few minutes, but I can't seem to get them out of my head."

"Or out of your heart, I suspect."

Nodding her head, Diana said, "Yeah, but...but it's more than that."

"How so?"

Pausing, Diana chewed nervously on her lip. Glancing at her aunt, she took a deep breath and said, "It's a woman."

Brenda's jaw dropped open and then closed just as quickly. Staring at her niece for a few seconds, the thinnest of smiles appeared on Brenda's face. Reaching over, she patted Diana on the knee and then rose to her feet. "I'm going to fix some more tea. Would you like some?"

"What? Um…sure," Diana said, handing Brenda her cup.

Heading to the kitchen, Brenda said, "Be right back."

"Wait. Aren't you going to say anything?"

"About what, dear?"

"About…well, about what I just said."

"Oh, that," Brenda replied, stopping by the doorway. "What would you like me to say?"

Dumbfounded by her aunt's casual attitude toward something Diana believed would be tantamount to a bombshell dropping, she shook her head. "I don't know. I…I just thought…I just thought that you'd have something to say."

Debating for only a second, the grin Brenda was trying to hide finally emerged. "Actually, I do."

Swallowing hard, Diana said, "Okay."

"The niece apparently doesn't fall far from the aunt."

Brenda watched for a few moments while Diana slowly caught up, and when she did, Brenda burst out laughing at her niece's flabbergasted expression. Without saying a word, Brenda turned on her heel and headed to the kitchen, her laughter continuing to echo through the house as she went.

***

After rapping lightly on the door, Linda walked into Jamie's office. "I was going to order some lunch. You hungry?"

Oblivious to Linda's existence, Jamie sat behind her desk with her chin resting on her hand as she focused on what she was writing.

Accustomed to Jamie's ability to concentrate when she was working, Linda merely rolled her eyes at being rebuffed. Walking over to the desk, she had intended to be quiet until Jamie noticed her, but when Linda saw what Jamie was scribbling on, she shouted, "Jamie! What in the world are you doing?"

Startled, Jamie looked up. "What?"

With a sigh, Linda pointed to the stack of papers on the desk. "Can I ask why you're writing all over those contracts? I did as you asked, and I'm fairly certain, I didn't miss anything."

Confused, Jamie lowered her eyes and when she saw her scrawl all over the cover page of one of the contracts, her shoulders fell. "Oh, shit."

"Oh, shit? Is that all you can say? I spent the better part of the morning getting them perfect."

"I'm sorry," Jamie said, sliding the papers in Linda's direction. "But it's only the top copy."

Unable to resist Jamie's charming pout, Linda let out a snort as she picked up the contracts, but when she saw what was written all over the cover page, she began to laugh. "What in the world is all of this?"

"I was just doodling."

"I've known you for almost thirty years, and have worked with you for nearly five, and in all of that time, you have never once *doodled*."

Tickled by Linda's motherly tone, Jamie asked, "How do you know? I could be a closet doodler."

"You're not a *closet* anything, and who's Diana?"

"What?"

"Diana," Linda said, pointing to the papers in her hand. "You've scribbled it a hundred times, along with what appears to be a…" Taking a moment to decipher Jamie's artistry, Linda said, "What is this? Holly?"

"No, mistletoe."

"Mistletoe?"

"Yes, mistle—" Stopping when she saw the befuddled look on Linda's face, Jamie began to laugh. Rocking back in her chair, she ran her fingers through her hair. "Christ, I'm acting like a goddamn teenager."

"What's going on? I've never known you to be so distracted at work, and I don't care what you say, you don't doodle."

"Can we please drop the doodling subject? It's becoming annoying," Jamie asked with a grin.

Chuckling, Linda nodded and sat down in one of the chairs opposite Jamie's desk. "Okay, out with it. What's got you so bothered that you doo…um…*draw* on freshly printed contracts?"

Jamie took a deep breath, and letting it out slowly, she said, "I met a woman."

"Oh, I see, and I'm assuming that her name is Diana?" Linda said, glancing at the papers in her hand.

"Yes. Diana Clarke," Jamie replied. "I met her at Phelan's party on—"

"Jamie, pardon me for interrupting, but you can do much better than those bimbos who date his clients."

"She's not one of those. She came with Gwen Fowler."

"Wait…that doesn't make sense. Gwen Fowler is straight, Jamie. She's got a husband."

"I know, but he was out of town, so Diana came along as company."

"And let me guess, you spent the entire evening talking to her."

"No, it was less than fifteen minutes."

"Fifteen minutes?" Linda said. Puzzled, she returned her attention to the scribbles Jamie had drawn on the contract. Biting her lip in order to prevent the widest smile she owned from appearing on her face, Linda said, "That may very well be a record for falling in love, I think."

"Love?" Jamie blurted. "Who said anything about love?"

"You did," Linda said, holding up the top page so Jamie could see it. "Unless I'm mistaken, Valentine's Day is in February. Therefore, the only explanation for all these hearts and arrows you've drawn amidst this field of mistletoe is love, unless, of course, you're thinking of getting into the greeting card business."

Knowing that Linda knew her better than she knew herself half the time, Jamie shook her head. "I don't suppose there's any point in denying this, is there?"

"Not a one," Linda said, knowingly. "Do you want to talk about it?"

"There's not that much to say. I met her. We had a drink, and we talked for a few minutes. That's all."

"But?"

With a sigh, Jamie said, "I can't get her out of my head, Linda. I can't. I've tried. Lord knows, I've tried, but it's no use. She's there to stay."

"So why do you sound so unhappy? I would think you'd be over-the-top ecstatic about meeting the woman of your dreams."

"I would be, if I hadn't been an ass and fucked it up."

Cocking her head to the side, Linda asked, "Care to explain?"

"Phelan was drunk out of his mind, and when Diana was about to leave, he stopped her at the door. There was some mistletoe hanging over it, and he wouldn't let her pass until she kissed him, so I stepped in and...and did the deed."

"And she was offended?"

"Actually, I don't know," Jamie said quietly, thinking back to when the kiss had ended. "She didn't say a word. She just walked out of the house without even a glance in my direction."

"Oh, I see," Linda said. "Well, I suppose that you could take it as a good sign that she didn't tell you off...or slap you in the face."

"Yeah, I guess. I'm just hoping she'll accept my apology. She told me that she was going to go to Lillian's party on Saturday night with Gwen, so that'll give me the chance to tell her that I'm sorry."

"Is that all you're going to say? Perhaps you should try telling her how you feel about her. You never know, she could feel the same way."

"Linda, the chances that Diana Clarke fell in love with me in a span of less than fifteen minutes is right up there with believing in Santa Claus. It's a wonderful idea, but it's hardly reality."

CHAPTER FOUR

"You're not ready?" Gwen asked. "Now there's a surprise."

"I'm sorry, but I won't be long. Come on up," Diana said with a guilty smile, running back up the stairs to her bedroom.

Sniggering at her friend's penchant for lateness, Gwen tossed her coat on a nearby chair, and climbed the stairs. Entering Diana's bedroom, she looked around and smiled.

"Someone went on a shopping spree," she said loudly, seeing several empty shopping bags tossed about.

"No, I just needed a few things," Diana called back from behind the bathroom door.

Picking up one of the bags, Gwen read the name imprinted on the side and jerked back her head. "Since when do you shop at Saks? A bit out of your budget, isn't it?"

"I wanted to get a new dress, and they were having a sale."

Noticing the name on another bag, Gwen called out, "And you needed new shoes because...no, let me guess. They were having a sale, too?"

"Actually, they were."

Accepting Diana's answer with a nod, Gwen smiled to herself as she picked up another bag, and when she saw the name of Joelliane stamped on the plastic, it was all she could do not to burst out laughing. Already having a sneaking suspicion that Diana's need for new clothes had nothing to do with bargain shopping and everything to do with a certain attractive blonde lawyer, it was all but confirmed seeing the packaging from the well-known lingerie store.

Sitting on the edge of the bed, Gwen tried to compose her mirth...along with her next sentence. Finally, she called out, "So, what you're saying is that none of this has anything at all to do with that lip-lock you shared with Jamie Nash?"

In the bathroom, Diana was leaning over the sink with her face close to the mirror as she applied her last bit of makeup. Hearing the question, she promptly poked herself in the eye with her eyeliner. "Shit," she said, blinking several times to clear the pain. Groaning at the site of the mess she just created, Diana grabbed a tissue and wiped away the swipe of black pencil from under her eye.

Hearing no response, Gwen said, "You okay in there?"

"Yes. Yes, I'm fine," Diana replied, quickly repairing the damage. "I'll be out in a minute."

Growing tired of shouting their conversation, Gwen waited until she heard the bathroom door open, and when she saw the dress Diana was wearing, her jaw dropped open. "Wow!"

"You like?" Diana asked as she felt her cheeks heat.

Gwen's eyes started at Diana's feet and slowly worked their way up, and then back down again. The dress was short, strapless, shimmering and very, very red. Pleated around the bust, with a wrapped skirt that was loose and flowing, it was beautiful. The addition of a small rhinestone brooch centered on the fabric between Diana's breasts added a hint of sparkle, and Diana did the rest. The swells of her breasts rose slightly above the pleats, helped, Gwen suspected, by a very expensive brassiere. The hem ended a few inches above her knees, allowing whoever was looking to get more than a hint of Diana's shapely legs, and at that moment in time, Gwen was looking…a lot.

"Well, what do you think?" Diana asked again, tickled by her friend's open-mouthed gape.

"Let's just put it this way," Gwen said, finally allowing her eyes to meet Diana's. "I just ogled you and I'm straight, so I think you might end up having to pick Jamison Nash up off the floor when she sees you in that."

Laughing at her friend's honesty, Diana's cheeks darkened yet another shade. Chewing on her lip for a second, Diana asked quietly, "Are you okay with this?"

Offering Diana a soft smile, Gwen said, "Attraction is fluid, Diana. I stood in Phelan's entry and watched her kiss you, and if the chemistry I saw was anywhere near what you felt, I'd say go for it."

Smiling wide, Diana said, "I feel like a schoolgirl going on her first date."

"Well, you sure as hell don't look like one," Gwen said with a chuckle. "Now come on, the *wo*man of your dreams is waiting."

***

As they traveled down the long, winding driveway leading to the Willoughby mansion, Diana had to blink to clear the spots from her eyes. Unlike Ted Phelan, Lillian Willoughby seemed to rejoice in the season to the point of being obnoxious. Her two-story house, including the four stately, round pillars in the front, had been completely outlined in red lights, while the front gardens seemed to have been infected by the diseases known as gaudy and glitz.

Figures of snowmen, outlined in blinking red LED lights, stood proudly in one area, while another was overflowing with penguins in blue and white. The next displayed a group of polar bears wearing red, blinking ribbons with their heads bobbing to some unknown tune, and the largest garden housed a collection of outrageously large LED green and red Christmas presents underneath a flashing banner spouting *Merry Christmas*.

"Oh my," Diana said, looking out the window of the car.

"In her defense, I'm fairly certain that she has four or five grandchildren."

"Well, I sure as hell hope Santa brings them sunglasses for Christmas. They're going to need them."

Chuckling as they climbed out of the car, they made their way up the arched stairs leading to the entry. Within seconds of ringing the bell, the door swung open.

"Merry Christmas," Lillian Willoughby said, giving the new arrivals her most brilliant smile, but as soon as she recognized Gwen Fowler, an underling in Lillian's small mind, she frowned. "Oh, it's just you. Well, you'd best get in here before all the heat escapes."

Walking into the home, Diana found herself surrounded by opulence, as well as enough shimmering and flashy Christmas decorations to put the LED explosion in the front yard to shame.

While the foyer was large and elegant, its beauty was marred by several tall, spiraled Christmas trees made entirely of gold and silver foil. Standing like twin sentries at each and every doorway, they silently rotated on stands, and as the branches reflected the light from the enormous chandelier overhead, a disco effect of dots and flickers of brilliance danced around the room. Adding to the flashy display was a thick rope of red garland that had been wound around the brass balustrade of the noble, curved stairway leading to the second floor. Dotted by green satin bows, it was coiled again and again around the handrail like a snake, winding its way toward its next victim.

Hearing the door close behind her, Diana turned and found Lillian Willoughby staring back at her.

"And who, may I ask, are you?" the woman asked, placing her hands on her hips. "You don't appear to be anyone I would know."

Annoyed by the woman's rudeness, but refusing to allow it to show, Diana put on her best smile and held out her hand. "I'm Diana Clarke. I'm a friend of Gwen's."

Narrowing her eyes, Lillian glanced from one woman to the other, studying each as if they had a clue that needed to be discovered. Pursing her lips, she limply shook Diana's outstretched hand and then looked in Gwen's direction. "What kind of friend...*exactly*?"

Like most large companies, Phelan, Willoughby and Nash had a grapevine filled with tidbits of information and amusing anecdotes about the partners of the firm. But while most were just rumors, one was not. Lillian Willoughby was as homophobic as the day was long.

Hoping to calm the woman's ruffled feathers, which were presently stuffed into an obscenely bright green dress, Gwen said quickly, "Diana's my best friend, Mrs. Willoughby. My husband is out of town, and since my invitation was for two, I asked Diana to come along. I hope you don't mind."

As if an invisible switch had been flipped, Lillian's frown turned into a beaming smile. "Of course not, Gwen. Now, get rid of those coats and start to mingle. Lots of important clients here tonight, so do your best to make them feel welcome. Remember, you're here representing Phelan, Willoughby and Nash."

Before Diana or Gwen could say another word, Lillian waddled across the shiny, white marble floor and disappeared through a large arched doorway.

"A bit full of herself, isn't she?" Diana said to Gwen, handing her coat to a waiting member of the house staff.

"You have no idea," Gwen said, rolling her eyes. "But unlike Phelan, Willoughby's taste in parties is a bit more upscale. Much better food and slightly better liquor."

"I thought you couldn't drink at these things, especially since you're here representing *Phelan, Willoughby and Nash*," Diana said, adding an air of snobbery to her tone.

"Don't remind me," Gwen said with a giggle, locking her arm through Diana's and leading her to the archway. "Now let's go see what's on the menu tonight."

***

After being introduced to all of Lillian's clients, and making the necessary small talk associated with corporate Christmas parties, Jamie had found the bar first and the patio second. To her dismay, Lillian's fondness for pageantry didn't stop at mere decorations. Several glass urns throughout the house had been filled with potpourri, and coupled with the smell of the bayberry-scented candles lining the mantle in the reception area, the fragrance had become overpowering. Within minutes of entering the home, Jamie's head began to pound, and soon after that, she began to sneeze.

Walking in from the patio for the umpteenth time, Jamie closed the door behind her and scanned the crowd again. While most of Lillian's clients were men in the process of getting a divorce, it seemed by the amount of women in the room, none of the men appeared to be grieving the loss of their wives. Paying no attention to those dressed in tuxedos, especially Ted Phelan, who was standing near a group of giggling women looking bored out of his mind, Jamie's eyes darted from one cocktail dress to the next. A few times she paused when dresses plunging low in the front or high on the thigh came into view, but when none of them were wrapped around the body belonging to Diana Clarke, she quickly lost interest. With a sigh, Jamie headed back to the bar. Exhausted from sneezing, and with her headache in full swing, she had resigned herself to the fact that her evening would have to end early.

As Gwen stopped to snag two glasses of Chablis from a waiter exiting the reception area, Diana continued inside. At first, she found herself impressed by the tall ceilings, and the fact that the room seemed to match the depth of the house, but when the smell of cloves, cinnamon and bayberry invaded her nostrils, Diana winced. Pushing past the pungent odor, she looked around and quickly came to the conclusion that Lillian Willoughby did *not* know the meaning of the word subdued.

Lengths of red garland, similar to the snake wrapped around the balustrade in the entry, had been draped over all the windows and doors, and animated snowmen and carolers swayed on every available windowsill. More gaudy Christmas-themed spangle shimmered, shined, blinked and twinkled all around the room, and the massive tree standing in the corner had been covered by hundreds of ornaments stuffed into every crevice of its artificial branches.

"Overkill comes to mind," Gwen whispered in Diana's ear as she came up behind her.

Turning around, Diana took the glass of wine from Gwen's hand. "Actually, I was thinking more along the lines of murder, but then I remembered the housing sucks."

Grinning, Gwen took a sip of wine and looked over Diana's shoulder at the throng of people milling about. Noticing one particular person, Gwen said, "You seemed to have captured someone's attention."

"Oh, please don't tell me it's Ted Phelan," Diana moaned, quickly tugging up the bodice of her dress.

"Somehow I don't think Phelan has ever filled out a tuxedo quite like that," Gwen replied. "And now, I'm going to mingle, and you're going to blush. Cheers." Giving Diana a wink, Gwen quickly disappeared into the crowd.

Swallowing hard, Diana took a deep breath and slowly turned around.

Being nearly six feet in height has its advantages. A bulb in a ceiling fixture can be easily changed without the need of a ladder. Items on the top shelves in grocery stores can be retrieved without so much as a stretch, and seeing over the heads of average-height women to spot the one you're looking for is effortless. Although miserable from her allergic reaction to the oppressive scent of dried flowers and herbs, when Jamie spotted Diana at the opposite end of the room, for a moment, her misery waned. As if on cue, the crowd slowly parted, and when Diana came into full view, the moisture in Jamie's mouth disappeared, and promptly reappeared somewhere else.

Gwen's description, although lacking in detail, was spot-on, and as Diana watched Jamie walk across the room, she couldn't help but admire the black tuxedo the woman was wearing. While most of the men at the party had also chosen to wear tuxedos, they lacked the panache of Jamie Nash. Choosing single or double-breasted suits with velvet collars and red or green cummerbunds, although appropriate for the occasion and for the season, they could have very easily been members of a men's choir waiting to perform. Jamie's tux, like the person who wore it, was unique. With no lapels on the jacket, it was simple, yet elegant. The mandarin collar and the piping down the edges of the coat were of black silk, as was the wing-collared shirt she wore underneath. However, unlike the others in the room wearing tuxedos, Jamie had chosen not to wear a tie, and she was fairly close to not wearing a shirt. Her black blouse was unbuttoned all the way down to where it met the candy-apple red vest which completed her ensemble, and the swells of her breasts were more than apparent in the glittering lights of the room.

Smiling as Jamie approached, Diana's expression suddenly turned to one of confusion when Jamie came to an abrupt halt several feet away. About to take a step in her direction, Diana stopped when Jamie held up her hand as if to say don't, and then watched in amusement as Jamie quickly squeezed her eyes shut, scrunched up her face, turned her head and sneezed.

Shaking it off, Jamie offered Diana an apologetic grin, but as she was about to speak, she sneezed again, and then again. Unable to say a word for fear that she'd spray the crowd with spittle, Jamie turned and ran outside, silently cursing Lillian Willoughby every step of the way.

Slightly amused by the alluring woman's demise into normality, Diana trotted after her. Grabbing a handful of cocktail napkins from a nearby table, she opened the French doors and walked out into the cold night air. With even more Christmas decorations lighting up the back of the house, it took her only a second to see Jamie standing near the railing. However, before Diana could say anything, Jamie sneezed again and then began to mumble.

"Fuck!" she growled as another sneeze rose from within and quickly escaped. Emptying the contents of her runny nose into a crumpled napkin, Jamie sniffled a few times and then sneezed again. "Fucking Willoughby and her fucking need to anoint the fucking house in dead flowers!"

Sneeze.

"God damn it!"

Sneeze.

"Oh, Jesus Christ, give me a fucking break!"

Sneeze.

Hearing someone giggling behind her, Jamie glanced over her shoulder and saw Diana standing near the door. "Christ, sorry. I didn't know anyone was out here."

Shaking her head, Diana walked over and handed Jamie the cocktail napkins. "I thought you might need these."

Quickly grabbing the wad of napkins, Jamie turned her back on Diana and blew her nose. Waiting a few seconds to make sure the tickle that had caused her sneezing had disappeared, Jamie turned back around. Noticing that Diana was trying not to laugh, Jamie asked, "You think this is funny?"

"No…well…maybe," Diana said, allowing one small snicker to escape. "You look funny when you sneeze?"

"I do?"

"Yeah, your face gets all scrunched up and…well, it's funny."

Before Jamie could respond, her nose tickled. Turning her back on Diana, Jamie sneezed again, and again, and again.

"God bless you," Diana said, putting her hand on Jamie's shoulder. "Are you all right?"

"Oh, Christ, that fucking potpourri is killing me," Jamie said, wiping her nose.

"Are you allergic to flowers?"

"No, but some perfumes get me going and that stench inside is stifling. It started just after I got here, but I didn't want to leave until I saw you," Jamie said, turning around.

"Oh."

"I wanted to apologize for what I did at Phelan's house. I had no right to force myself on you. I was enjoying your company, and I think I ruined the evening by doing what I did."

"You wanted Phelan to kiss me?"

"What? No! Of course not."

"Then I don't think you have anything to apologize for."

"You're not angry?"

Of all the emotions that Diana had felt since meeting Jamie Nash, anger had yet to make the list. Surprise had struck the first night they had met, both at the jacket offered and Diana's own reaction to the chivalrous gesture. Trust quickly followed when Jamie came to her rescue under the mistletoe, and anticipation began to heat her blood a few days later when she found herself walking through shops looking for the perfect dress with only one person in mind. Fear crept onto the scene as she stood in the bathroom repairing her makeup earlier that night, wondering if what she was feeling was real. And it was that feeling…that *emotion*…that was doing her head in. How could she be feeling love for someone she didn't even know? She had never been in love before. In lust – yes. Intrigued – yes. Infatuated – most definitely, but what she was feeling for Jamie seemed to be more than all of those combined. Much more.

Brought back to the conversation by a slight breeze that sent a chill down her spine, Diana said, "Of course I'm not angry."

Smiling at Diana's response, and the fact that her sneezing fit had finally ended, Jamie wadded up the napkins and stuffed them in a nearby flowerpot. Taking a deep breath of the crisp air, she reached into her pocket to find her cigarettes.

Taking a moment to admire the way Jamie's tuxedo was tailored to fit her womanly curves, Diana broke the silence. "Nice suit, by the way."

"Thank you," Jamie said, bowing her head at the compliment. After lighting her cigarette, she casually exhaled and allowed herself the pleasure of taking in the sight of Diana Clarke. While Jamie had told her eyes *not* to stop at the dark valley between Diana's breasts, her eyes apparently had a mind of their own. After lingering there for a few seconds, she was finally able to force them upward, and when she looked into Diana's eyes, Jamie said in a breath, "Awesome dress."

The flutter that Jamie's throaty whisper had caused meandered its way through Diana's body and settled soundly between her legs with a thud. Fighting the urge to close her eyes and relish in the feel of it, Diana took a deep, ragged breath, hoping that the crisp night air could somehow extinguish the fire Jamie had just ignited.

"Christ, you've got to be freezing," Jamie said suddenly, hearing Diana's shaky intake of breath. "You should go back inside."

"Will you come with me?"

"Are you sure you want to risk it? I'm out of cocktail napkins. It could get quite messy."

Grinning, Diana said, holding out her hand, "I'll take my chances."

Dropping the cigarette to the patio, Jamie ground it out and took Diana's hand. It felt good. It felt right. It felt amazing.

CHAPTER FIVE

"Why am I not surprised?" Diana said as Jamie walked toward her carrying an open bottle of wine and two glasses.

"Well, you didn't expect me to drink the swill that Lillian serves, did you?"

"Are you a wine snob?"

"No, but I prefer the ones with corks rather than screw caps."

"Oh, you *are* a snob."

"I like what I like," Jamie said softly, handing Diana a glass. "It's a Cabernet."

As she brought the glass to her lips, Diana could smell a hint of black cherry and cocoa, and taking a sip, she smiled softly at the flavors of black licorice swirling with the oakiness of the wine.

"It's delicious."

"Thanks," Jamie said, taking a seat. Glancing at Diana for a moment, Jamie settled back and crossed her legs. Although the pounding between her temples brought on by the potpourri hadn't diminished, the sneezing that had plagued her for over an hour had finally disappeared. Taking a relaxing breath, Jamie took a sip of wine and asked, "So, Diana Clarke, tell me...who are you?"

"What?" Diana replied, snickering.

Shrugging her shoulders, Jamie said, "All I know is that you're Gwen's friend."

"What do you want to know?" Diana asked, keeping her eyes locked on Jamie's as she brought the wineglass to her lips. "But remember, I get to ask you the same questions."

Nodding her head, Jamie thought for a moment. "Okay, we'll start with something not too taxing. How about...what do you do for a living?"

"I was a prison officer."

"You work in a prison?" Jamie blurted.

"Does that surprise you?"

"A little."

"Why?" Diana asked, settling back in her chair and crossing her legs.

Unable to resist, Jamie stole a quick glance of Diana's nicely-formed calves before raising her eyes and finding Diana smiling back at her. Remembering what Diana had asked, Jamie said, "I guess I always thought that prison officers were a bit more…um…*burly*."

"Well, there are a few like that, but it's not a prerequisite for the job."

Allowing herself the pleasure of taking in the view of Diana's shapely legs one more time, it took several seconds before their eyes met again. Raising an eyebrow, Jamie smiled. "Obviously not."

Inwardly, Diana sighed at the woman's sexual tone. Swallowing the moisture building in her mouth, Diana drank some wine to wash it down.

"Wait. You said you *were* a prison officer? You aren't now?" Jamie asked.

"No, I resigned my position a few weeks ago."

"Can I ask why?"

"I actually started as a teacher, but when budget cuts came along, they did away with most of the classes offered to the prisoners. Since I already had the training to be an officer, I took the job when it was offered. Unfortunately, the difference I thought I was making by teaching the women skills in the classroom all but stopped as soon as I put on the uniform, so I took my non-burly self and called it a day," Diana said with a grin.

"So what now?"

"Well, I still have a teaching degree, so I'm hoping I can find a position in one of the youth offender programs. Maybe, in my own small way, I can actually help a few of them realize that there's more to this world than just gangs and drugs."

"So you still want to make a difference then?"

"Yes, I do."

"Admirable."

Deciding it was time to turn the tables, Diana said, "Speaking of admirable, since I already know what you do for a living, Gwen told me that you do a lot of pro bono work. Can I ask why?"

"Because it keeps me grounded."

"How so?"

"I live in a world of corporations and three-piece suits, where the higher-ups take home bonuses in the millions, while sometimes forgetting that there are people below them that struggle to make ends meet. I don't ever want to be like that. I'm not saying that a free turkey at Christmas or some spare change dropped into a basket doesn't help, because it does, but sometimes people need more than that. Sometimes they need a bit of guidance, or knowledge, or just a little help understanding words they don't know."

"And that's where you come in?"

With a nod, Jamie said, "It started when I was in law school. I knew my father volunteered his time, and one summer he asked if I'd like to clerk for him on some of the pro bono stuff. Eager beaver that I was, I agreed, and before too long, I was there even when he wasn't. And now, he helps me."

"Wait. I thought your father retired?"

"He retired from the firm, but not from the law. He still practices, only now he does it for free," Jamie said with a grin.

"It sounds like you like working with him."

"I do, very much. He's a brilliant man, and we both love being able to help people in need."

"So if you love it so much, why not do it full-time?"

"Because I like nice things," Jamie said as she refilled their wine glasses. "I like fancy cars and living in the country, and being able to afford to go on vacation wherever I'd like. My position at the firm gives me the opportunity to live the life I want, while helping those that I can. It's the best of both worlds, and I wouldn't want to give up either."

"Even though you work with Phelan and Willoughby?"

Rolling her eyes, Jamie chuckled. "I've learned to take them both with a very large grain of salt. Since we have our own divisions, our paths don't often cross, and when they do, let's just say I try to leave my personal feelings at the door. My work is far too important to me to let their idiosyncrasies get in the way. It's not a match made in heaven, but it's doable."

"You're amazing," Diana said in a breath.

The sultry tone forced Jamie to shift in her seat, and taking a taste of wine, she waited for the throbbing between her legs to subside. Managing to find her voice a few seconds later, she said, "I'm just me."

"I like just you," Diana said, and then instantly blushed when she realized that the words she was thinking had just slipped from her lips. Swallowing hard, she quickly changed the subject. "Do you have any brothers or sisters?"

"Um…yes. I have a younger sister, Stacy."

"Is she a lawyer, too?"

"No, a photographer," Jamie said. "How about you? Any siblings?"

"No. Just me"

"Well, then tell me something about your parents. What do they do?"

"Oh, um…they died when I was four. A car accident."

"Christ, I'm sorry."

Offering Jamie a soft smile, Diana said, "Thanks. It was a long time ago, and I have only hazy memories of them now. My father's sister, Brenda, raised me."

"She did a great job."

"You think?"

"Absolutely," Jamie replied, gazing into Diana's eyes.

Smiling back at Jamie, Diana was about to ask for more wine when she saw Jamie's face scrunch up as another sneeze came over her. Before Diana could say a word, Jamie was out of her chair and heading back outside.

"Shit," Diana said under her breath, getting to her feet.

"Oh, this is getting fucking ridiculous!" Jamie bellowed, trying to hold back the sneeze that was forming. "Please…not again."

Sneeze.

"Crap!"

Sneeze

"Enough!"

Sneeze

"Oh, someone just kill me now."

"That would be a waste of a very good woman, I think," Diana said, coming up to stand next to Jamie. "Here, I brought you more napkins."

"Thanks," Jamie said.

Waiting until Jamie blew her nose a few times, Diana finally asked, "You doing better?"

Jamie turned and was about to reply, but the words got stuck in her throat. Between the moonlight and the Christmas lights strung here and there, Diana was awash in a soft, white glow, and she was breathtaking. Her hair shimmered in the light, and while the valley between her breasts was dark, the swells rising above the fabric were like porcelain.

"Jamie, are you okay?"

Snapped from her thoughts by Diana's voice, Jamie quickly removed her coat. "Here take this, you must be freezing."

"I'll be okay. You need it," Diana said, pushing the jacket away.

"No, I don't," Jamie said, holding it open. "Between all the sneezing and the sight of you in that dress, trust me, the last thing I need is this coat."

She hadn't meant for her feelings to slip out so easily, but once they had there was no turning back. The flirting had been fun, but somewhere along the way, it had turned into something more for Jamie, and she needed to know if the feeling was mutual. When she saw Diana's smile, Jamie got her answer…and her heart began to race.

Taking a deep breath, Diana turned around, placing her arms into the jacket as Jamie wrapped it around her, and for a moment they were in each other's arms. The wool smelled of crisp cologne and cigarettes, and the red silk lining, already heated by the woman behind her, felt warm against Diana's skin. Closing her eyes, Diana breathed in the moment, committing it to memory, and praying it would be the first of many.

Feeling Diana relax against her, Jamie sighed. Intentionally lowering her mouth to Diana's ear, she whispered, "Warm enough?"

The feel of Jamie's breath on her cheek caused Diana's body to quiver with need. Swallowing hard, she opened her eyes and turned around. Even in the muted light, Diana could see the passion in Jamie's eyes, but there was also a hint of mischief. Deciding to turn the tables, Diana purred back, "I'm getting hotter by the minute. How about you?"

Snickering, Jamie replied, "If we keep this up, I'm going to get a tan."

Diana laughed, and while the seductive mood was broken, the feelings were not.

"You want to stay out here for a while?" Diana asked.

Breathing in the fresh air, Jamie nodded her head. "At least for a few minutes, if you don't mind?"

"No, not at all," Diana said. While Jamie disposed of the used napkins in a planter, Diana walked over and looked out across the back yard. Brick-edged gardens dotted the lawn, and each was filled with animated figures of snowmen, penguins, polar bears and reindeer.

"Extraordinary, isn't it?" Jamie said, coming over to stand by her side.

A bit disappointed that Jamie seemed to like the overblown decorations, Diana asked, "Do you really like it?"

"I was being facetious. I can't stand all this stuff."

"You don't like Christmas?"

"What? No, that's not what I mean. I adore Christmas. I just don't like it when people placard their properties with all this crap. It's like they're in some sort of competition to see who can use the most electricity."

"I totally agree."

"Fuck!"

Surprised by Jamie's outburst, Diana looked up just as Jamie sneezed again, and then again.

"Oh, damn it all to hell," Jamie growled, fumbling in her pockets for a napkin. Taking a few steps away, she sneezed a few more times and then hung her head in defeat.

"You okay?" Diana asked.

Running her fingers through her hair, Jamie said with a sigh, "I'm afraid this isn't going to stop, and my head feels like it's about to explode. I'm sorry."

"What? Why didn't you tell me you had a headache?"

"Because I didn't want to ruin the evening. I thought it would go away, but I'm afraid that ridiculous potpourri has done me in." Stopping as the pain between her temples pulsed again, Jamie said sadly, "I'm sorry, but I really think I need to go."

"Don't apologize. It's okay. We can continue this later."

"We can?"

"Well, if you've invited Gwen to your party, I'll see you then," Diana said, smiling.

Returning the grin, Jamie said, "I did, and I can't wait."

"Then it's settled," Diana said as she removed the tuxedo jacket and handed it back to Jamie. "Now, let's get you out of here so you can take care of that headache."

Across the room, Lillian Willoughby watched as Jamie and Diana walked back inside, pursing her lips in disgust at the sight. Up until that moment, Lillian hadn't recognized Diana as the woman who Jamie had kissed at Ted Phelan's house, and now that she had, her party mood was quickly being replaced by that of disdain. Watching as they walked toward the entrance hall, Lillian's first thought was *good riddance*, but when she noticed something hanging over the archway, her eyes bulged.

Having always believed that public displays of affection were unnecessary and offensive, Lillian Willoughby had never adorned any of the doorways in her house with mistletoe during the Christmas season. Seeing that someone had taken it upon themselves to hang a sprig of the aphrodisiacal weed in her home, her temper fired instantly. While she may well have tolerated a playful smooch between those of the opposite sex in her home, Lillian had no tolerance for homosexuality. In her mind, it was loathsome. Angrily pushing her way through her guests, she marched to the door in her sequined, open-toed pumps.

Walking through the room, Diana had unconsciously held out her hand, and in an instant, she felt Jamie's fingers mesh with hers. Smiling all the way to the doorway, they both stopped and waited as other guests were helped on and off with their coats. Their eyes met for a moment, and then all of a sudden, a voice rang out.

"None of that, Nash. Not in my house."

Furrowing her brow, Jamie glanced as Lillian approached. "What was that?"

"You know very well I don't appreciate your kind," Lillian scolded, glaring first at Jamie and then at Diana. Pointing to the front door, she said, "Don't let it hit you on your way out, and make sure you take your *friend* with you."

"You're way out of line, Lillian," Jamie growled under her breath. "We were just talking."

Wrinkling up her face in disgust, Lillian pointed to the mistletoe hanging above the two women. "Do I look like I was born yesterday? You put that mistletoe there so you could have a repeat performance of what happened at Ted's last week. Well, not in my house, missy."

Glancing up, Jamie couldn't help but smile at the sight of the seasonal decoration, and then returned her attention to Lillian Willoughby. Even though her head was pounding, Jamie couldn't resist pushing a few of Lillian's buttons.

"What? You mean you didn't put it there for me?"

With her face getting redder by the minute, Lillian said, "Like that would ever happen. Now, take it down!"

"I'm not the one that hung it there, Lillian."

"I've been around too long to believe that you didn't."

"Well, they do say miracles happen at Christmas."

"Miracles, my foot," Lillian said, eyeing her business partner from top to bottom. "Your kind doesn't believe in miracles."

Diana stood there and listened to the exchange, all the while fighting the urge to punch Lillian Willoughby squarely on the jaw.

The woman was clearly homophobic. The woman was wrong, *and* the woman was being extremely rude. Seeing the flush of embarrassment creep across Jamie's face, Diana didn't have to think twice. Taking one step forward, she reached up and pulled Jamie's face to hers, and as Lillian Willoughby gasped in shock, Diana kissed Jamie solidly on the lips.

Just like their first kiss, when their lips touched, both were again lost in the flavors and the feel. Unconsciously, Jamie placed her hand on Diana's shoulder, and the naked, creamy skin beneath her fingers was so warm and smooth, Jamie's libido lurched. Her mind became a hurricane of images, swirling flickers of nights filled with passion, moans and gasps, and relaxing into the kiss, she drank every ounce of it in. It was to die for.

For the past week, Diana had tried to convince herself that her memories of their first kiss had been tainted by her imagination, warping reality into something divine. Now, with Jamie's mouth pressed against hers again, she knew that she had been wrong. Jamie *was* divine…no doubt about it. Diana's blood began to boil. Between her legs was born an ache that she knew only Jamie could soothe, and it took all the strength she had not to open her lips and beg for Jamie's tongue to enter. Feeling a moan of passion rising from within, Diana sighed as she pulled out of the kiss. Slowly running her fingers across the shoulders of Jamie's jacket to remove non-existent lint, she smiled up at the woman whose brilliant blue eyes had turned almost black with desire.

Lowering her voice to a whisper only Jamie could hear, Diana said, "I don't know about you, but I believe in miracles."

***

Reading yet another letter in a long line of letters, Santa stopped suddenly and wrinkled his nose. "Good Lord, what is that smell?"

"I'm afraid it's me, sir," Percy said meekly as he chimed and tinkled his way into the room.

Smiling at the sight of the little elf, Santa said, "Well, now, I know that I sent you to a party, but I didn't know it was being held in a perfume factory."

"It's potpourri, sir. I can't seem to rid myself of the smell."

"A bit over-the-top, isn't it?"

"Yes, sir, but the lady who was holding the party...well, she was a bit over-the-top herself."

"I see," Santa said, taking off his reading glasses. "So, tell me, how did it go?"

Two dimples appeared on Percy's cheeks as the tiny elf smiled from one pointed ear to the other. Climbing into a chair, he said, "I'm not positive, but I think it went well."

"You think?"

"Well, they kissed again. Miss Diana and Miss Jamie, that is."

"Jamie?"

"That's what she likes to be called, sir"

"Percy, were you eavesdropping?"

"Me, sir?" Percy said, blushing slightly. "No, sir...well, I mean, I tried not to, but...but I couldn't help but overhear a few things. They were too close not to."

"I see. So, what else did you hear?"

"They just talked about their work and their families. Miss Jamie was having an issue with the potpourri in the room, so she ended up having to leave early, but not before they shared a kiss under our mistletoe, sir."

"And that went well, I'm assuming," Santa asked. Watching as the small man's cheeks turned the color of Rudolph's nose, Santa let out a hearty laugh. "Apparently, it did."

"Yes, sir," Percy said as his cheeks turned a few shades darker. "It went really well."

CHAPTER SIX

"What do you mean, you're not going!"

Looking around the shopping mall's food court at the heads turning in the direction of their table, Gwen said, "You do realize that you're screaming. Don't you?"

"I am?" Diana said, lowering her voice. "I'm sorry, but didn't you say you had to attend *all* the parties?"

"Yes, I was supposed to, but I got dispensation for Jamie's since Adam and I will be out of town visiting his parents."

"But you're not leaving until the twenty-third."

"That's right, and Jamie's party is on Christmas Eve."

"Christmas Eve!" Diana shouted. Gwen's cringe got Diana's attention, and looking around, she saw at least a dozen shoppers gawking in her direction. Lowering her voice, Diana leaned closer to her friend. "What is she doing having a party on Christmas Eve? That doesn't make any sense."

"I have no idea," Gwen said, taking a bite of her salad. "But that's what the invitation said, and as soon as I saw the date, I called her assistant, Linda. I explained the situation, and was excused from making an appearance."

Diana's shoulders drooped. "Oh, I told her that I'd be there," she said quietly.

"I'm sure she wouldn't mind if you showed up without me. She'd probably appreciate it. Having you all to herself, so to speak."

"That's not the problem."

"No?"

"Gwen, I'm leaving for Burlington on the twenty-*second*."

"Oh, I forgot about that, but I'm sure Jamie will understand. Like you said, it's Christmas Eve, and normally people do have a tendency to spend that night with their families."

Diana's appetite disappeared, and putting down her fork, she sighed. "I suppose."

"Look, just call her up. Tell her that you'll be out of town, and you'll get in touch with her when you get back. What's the problem?"

"I…I just wanted to see her again, that's all."

Studying her friend for a second, Gwen leaned over, and touched the back of Diana's hand. "You've really fallen for her, haven't you?"

Taking a deep breath, Diana nodded her head. "Yes, I have."

Thinking for a moment, Gwen grabbed her handbag off the floor. Removing a small wad of papers, she shuffled through them and then slid an ivory-colored parchment envelope across the table. "That's the invitation."

"I just told you, I can't go."

"I know, but it's got her direct number on it, so you don't have to go through the switchboard. Now, how about we finish our lunch, and our shopping, and then head back to yours? That way, you can call her this afternoon, and we can spend the night wrapping our presents like we planned."

"Thanks," Diana said, picking up the envelope and putting it in her bag.

"Diana, it's not the end of the world. She'll understand. Trust me."

***

With two mugs of coffee in one hand, and a folder tucked under her arm, Linda stopped at the window to gaze at the snow rapidly covering the city. Smiling, she tapped on Jamie's door and walked inside.

"It seems you got your wish," she stated, placing a mug on the desk. "It's snowing like crazy out there, and they say it's not going to let up for a few days."

"Yes, I know," Jamie said, taking a sip of coffee. "Isn't it great!"

"Great, my eye. You have people to shovel *your* walks."

"Linda, you know I can arrange—"

"Oh stop," Linda said, waving off Jamie's offer. "You're as bad as your father. I don't need any help. I'm just complaining because…because at my age that's what you're supposed to do when it snows. Personally, I adore the stuff."

"Could have fooled me."

"Apparently, I did," Linda said with a snort. "I've got to tell you, when you came up with this idea of yours, I thought you had lost your mind."

Grinning, Jamie said, "I know."

"You are by far the soppiest person at Christmas I've ever known. You even surpass your father."

"That bad, eh?"

Rising to her feet, Linda walked around the desk and placed a small kiss on Jamie's cheek. "No…that good." Placing the folder on the desk, she said, "This is the final list of those who can't attend. Due to it being on Christmas Eve, as expected, there are a few that can't make it, but you'll still have a full house."

"Tell me that Phelan and Willoughby are included in this list and I'll love you forever."

"You're not that lucky, I'm afraid."

"Damn," Jamie said, opening the folder. Reading down the neatly typed list of names, her head jerked up. "Linda, this can't be right. Gwen Fowler is on here."

"That's right. She had to cancel. Something about being out of town. Her name was on the list I gave you last week. Didn't you see it?"

"No, to tell you the truth, I never looked at it. Too busy doing other things," Jamie said. Slumping in her chair, she shook her head. "She blew me off."

"Who?"

"Diana. She said she was coming to the party with Gwen, but obviously that's not the case."

"I thought you and she were getting along marvelously?"

"So did I," Jamie said, tossing the folder across her desk. "Apparently, I was wrong."

Saddened by the look on Jamie's face, Linda said, "Maybe she didn't know that Gwen wasn't going to be there. I mean, I don't tell my friends all my plans."

"I suppose."

"Why don't you just give her a call and invite her personally, then you'll know for sure."

"I don't have her number."

"Well, that's certainly not like you."

"She told me she'd be there, and I believed her," Jamie said, rocking back in her chair.

Reaching over, Linda moved Jamie's laptop to the edge of the desk. Tapping her fingers over the keys, she asked, "How does she spell it?"

"Spell what?" Jamie asked, looking up. "What in the world are you doing?"

"I'm doing an Internet search. Now, how does she spell her last name? With or without an e?"

"I have no idea."

Taking a deep breath, Linda said, "Well, I do enjoy a challenge. Let's see what I can find."

A few minutes passed before Linda moved the laptop back to its original position. "It appears that between the two spellings, there are twenty-seven Diana Clarkes in New York alone. Of course, that doesn't include those who prefer not to have their number listed, or those living in Jersey or Connecticut. Do you know if she lives in the city?"

Still feeling like she had been played, Jamie sighed. "It doesn't matter. I wouldn't call her anyway."

"What are you talking about? You like this woman."

"She lied to me."

"Jamie, it's not like you to be this way. Why don't you just go find Gwen, get Diana's number, and give her a call?"

"No," Jamie said, crossing her arms. "I've got five days until the party, and I have too much to do to spend my time chasing some bitch that lied to me."

"Jamie—"

"You know what?" Jamie said, looking at her watch. "It's almost three. Pack up your things. We're getting out of here."

"What?"

Reaching over, Jamie switched her phone to the answering machine and closed her laptop. "What I need to do, I can do from home. You've already got Monday off, so enjoy your extended weekend, and I'll see you on Tuesday."

"Jamie, I know you're hurting right now. It's as plain as the nose on your face, but you're not being rational. This is just a misunderstanding. I'm sure of it."

"You don't even know her."

"And neither do you! Don't assume the worst. It's not fair to you, and it's certainly not fair to her."

"She lied to me!"

"Oh, I can't stand it when you act like that stubborn little girl you used to be. It infuriates me!"

"I'm not being stubborn!"

"No, you're being stupid!" Linda shouted, placing her hands on her hips. "Jamie, I have known you since you were six years old and I know when you're scared, and right now, you're terrified."

"You don't know what you're talking about."

"Jamison, you're in love. You've fallen for this woman, and it scares you, because all of a sudden, nothing else matters. I know you Jamie, and I know that the thought of not seeing her is driving you crazy, and you've channeled your frustration into this...this...this stupid idea that she lied to you."

"She did."

"Oh, Jesus Christ, Jamison, you're acting like a child!"

Shoving her chair away from her desk, Jamie stood up and glared at Linda. "No, I'm not, because children believe in Santa Claus, Linda, and I *don't*!"

***

Looking up from his cup of hot chocolate, Santa smiled as Percy scampered into the dining room.

"You wanted to see me, sir?" he said as he approached the table.

Motioning toward a chair, Santa said, "Sit down, Percy. We need to talk."

Sensing a bit of foreboding in Santa's tone, Percy grew worried. Keeping one eye on the man in the red suit, Percy pulled out a chair and hopped onto the seat.

"It seems we might have a bit of a problem," Santa said.

"A...a...problem, sir?"

Momentarily forgetting that his lead elf was also his most nervous elf, when Santa realized his mistake, he shook his head. "Relax, Percy, you haven't done anything wrong."

"I haven't, sir?" Percy said, his voice raising an octave.

Amused, Santa asked, "I don't know, have you?"

"What? No...no, sir. Of course not, sir. Well, other than the small detail about Miss Diana's letter in the sack lining, but we've taken care of that, or we will after I deliver the last sprig of mistletoe."

"Actually, that's why I called for you. It seems that the last party our Diana is supposed to attend is not on the twenty-first as we were told."

"It's not, sir?"

"No, apparently He has a new secretary, and she misread His handwriting. I received an e-mail from Him this morning with the correction. It seems that Jamison Nash's party is on the twenty-fourth."

Tilting his head to the side, Percy asked, "The twenty-fourth?"

"That's right," Santa said, waiting for the elf to catch up. It didn't take long.

"*The twenty-fourth*!" Percy shouted as he jumped from his chair. "Why...why...why...why that's Christmas Eve, sir! I can't deliver mistletoe on Christmas Eve, sir. My job is sitting on the sleigh with you. Helping you deliver the gifts. It's what I work for. It's what I wait for. It's what I live for!"

"I know that, Percy, which is why I called you in here," Santa said, watching as Percy climbed back onto his chair. "You and I have a decision to make."

"We do, sir?"

"Yes, we do. As I see it, we have three options. The first is that I send another elf in your place to deliver the mistletoe."

"But no one else has traveled by themselves, sir. They always go in groups, except for me, that is."

"Yes, I know," Santa said. "The next option would be for us to forego the placement of the last sprig, and concentrate on our deliveries for Christmas Eve. We can't forget that there are millions of children depending on us, so if one wish never gets granted, that's the way it will have to be."

"I don't like that option, sir," Percy said quietly, shaking his head.

"No?"

"No, sir. Every child gets a wish granted. That's the rule. We can't break the rule, sir."

"You forget. Miss Diana isn't a child anymore."

"But she never got her wish! You can't go with option number two, sir. You just *can't*."

Nodding his head, Santa said, "Well, then…there's only one other option, isn't there?"

Tears formed in Percy's eyes as he realized what Santa was saying. Swallowing back his emotions, the little man took a ragged breath, and then straightening his backbone, sat proud and tall in his chair. "I'll deliver it, sir. As lead elf it's my duty to see a job through to the end, no matter what the cost."

"Are you sure, Percy? I know how much Christmas Eve means to you."

"I'm sure, sir, because while you're granting the wishes of the children, I will be granting one for an adult. It's a first, I believe, yes?"

Smiling, Santa said, "Yes, Percy, it is a first."

Jumping off the chair, Percy took a deep breath and straightened his jacket. "Well, then, I'd best go plan for my trip. May I be excused?"

"Of course."

Watching as Percy shuffled across the room, Santa called out, "Percy!"

Turning around, Percy replied, "Yes, sir."

"Make sure you have some eggnog at the party."

Smiling, Percy nodded his head. "Will do, sir…and I'll have a cup for you as well."

"You do that, my friend. You do that."

***

"Any luck?" Gwen asked, walking into the lounge.

Setting her cell phone on the coffee table, Diana said, "No, I just keep getting a message that the line is out of order. Must be the storm."

"Yeah, well, it's getting rather nasty out there," Gwen said as she sat down. "Did you run an Internet search?"

"Yes, but her home number isn't listed," Diana said with a sigh as she leaned back into the sofa. "I guess I'll just have to wait until Monday when she gets back to the office—"

"Diana, she won't be in on Monday."

"Why?"

"She's on vacation until after the first."

"Shit! This just keeps getting better and better."

"Calm down," Gwen said with a snicker. "I'm sure the phones will be working soon, so just keep trying and when you get through, leave her a message. Since it's the number she put on the invitation, I'm sure she'll be checking it. I know it's not the same as talking to her in person, but it's better than nothing."

Drumming her fingers on the sofa, Diana thought about her options. "No, I'm not calling her."

"Why the hell not? I thought you liked her."

"I do."

"Then for God's sake, call her. Don't just stand her up. That's not like you."

Seeing that Diana was retrieving her mobile from the coffee table, Gwen said, "Thank goodness you've come to your senses. Just leave her a message—"

"I'm not calling Jamie," Diana interrupted as she scrolled through the contact list on her phone. "I'm calling Brenda."

"Why?"

"To tell her I won't be up for Christmas."

"Hallelujah!" Gwen screamed as she reached over and squeezed Diana's arm. "I swear to God, Diana, if you hadn't just said that, I was going to take you by the shoulders and shake some sense into you!"

"Really? I'm not being stupid?"

"Diana, hand me the phone. I'll dial the number for you."

***

Returning from the kitchen with another bottle of wine, Gwen asked, "Well, how'd your aunt take it?"

"She's fine and wished me luck."

"You told her about Jamie?" Gwen asked as she sat on the floor next to a pile of wrapping paper and bows.

"Yeah, when I went up for Joanie's baby shower."

"She's okay with it?"

"Apparently, she's gay."

"Joanie's gay?"

"Not my cousin, my aunt."

"Your aunt Brenda is gay!"

"Yep."

"When the hell did that happen?"

Laughing at the wide-eyed look of surprise on Gwen's face, Diana said, "Do you remember me telling you about a woman named Susan?"

"Susan?" Gwen said, searching her memory. "Susan. Susan. Sus—oh, you mean the one that leases the apartment over your aunt's gar—age."

"That's the one."

"They're lovers?"

"Yep."

"She told you that?"

"Yep."

"Can you say something other than yep?"

"Yep," Diana said with a giggle.

Sending her friend a playful sneer, Gwen said, "Seriously, Diana, how did she keep it a secret for so long...and why?"

"She told me that she was afraid that Joanie and I would suffer if people found out. She didn't come to terms with it until she and Uncle David had been divorced for a few years, and then she met Susan, and they fell in love. So, Susan rented the apartment so they could close without anyone suspecting anything."

"Didn't Susan move out a few years ago?"

"Yeah. Brenda said that she got tired of waiting for her to come out, but it sounds like they're getting back together, which is the reason that Brenda finally admitted it to Joanie and I."

"Joanie knows?"

"Yes, Brenda told her a few months ago, but she was waiting until she could tell me face-to-face."

"Wow."

"Tell me about it," Diana said, chuckling as she refilled her wineglass. "Here I was thinking that my aunt was this prim and proper schoolteacher, and all the while she was banging a librarian over the garage."

***

When Jamie arrived home, she refused to allow her bruised heart to rule her mood. Pushing her disappointment aside, she focused on the task at hand. After calling all the vendors to make sure everything was in order for Christmas Eve, she changed into a pair of jeans and a red T-shirt, and in socked feet, began decorating her house. Asking only that her staff pile the totes of decorations in the main hall before they left for the evening, alone in her home, Jamie set about hanging the lights and garland. Amidst the smell of the pine tree delivered that morning, and the sounds of Christmas carols playing on the stereo, she worked into the night. It wasn't until her stomach complained, that she finally put the decorations aside and padded to the kitchen to find something to eat. Afterward, with her belly full, she grabbed a bottle of wine and retired to the solitude of her library to have a smoke.

In a room lit only by the glow coming from the fireplace, Jamie sat behind her desk of cherry. Watching the cigarette smoke float through the air, she groaned as her body pulsed again. "Shit," she whispered to the empty room.

Jamie had made a mistake, and she knew it. She had opened a bottle of Cabernet, and the taste of the wine brought back the flavors of a kiss. No longer able to hide from the memories and the desires that raged within her, she closed her eyes and allowed her thoughts to run wild.

In only a matter of minutes, her breathing began to change. Lazy breaths morphed into short gasps as she imagined what it would be like to caress the woman of her dreams. To kiss her. To hold her...and to taste her.

With a sigh, Jamie unzipped her jeans and lazily slid her hand inside, and a husky moan slipped from her lips as her fingers brushed over her trimmed curls. Snaking her fingers through folds, thick and wet, she closed her eyes and caressed herself as visions of Diana appeared in her mind. Shifting in her seat, Jamie moved her fingers lower, and tentative in her exploration, like that of a lover not yet as accomplished as herself, she tickled her entrance, a soft smile gracing her face at the feel of the moistness flowing from her center.

As her mind conjured up another image of Diana, Jamie's inner walls pulsed, and letting out a throaty purr, she began to rub her most sensitive erogenous zone. Moving her fingers slowly over the nub, she sighed in the darkness as she felt it begin to grow and thrive. The rhythm she set was gentle at first. Applying just enough pressure to make her juices flow, but not enough to cause release to come too soon, with skilled fingers, Jamie worked her body until her breathing grew labored and sweat covered her brow.

With a grunt, she rose to her feet long enough to push her jeans to the floor, and gasping for air, she returned to the leather chair, its surface now heated and damp. Running her finger over her clit for only a moment, she moved lower, and entering herself, Jamie pushed her finger in as far as it would go. "Yes," she hissed, flexing her hips to receive all that she could. "Oh, God...yes."

In and out she drew her finger, teasing herself by sliding it over her sensitive womanly nub for a few seconds, before plunging inside again and arching against the impalement. No longer wanting to hold off the inevitable, her strokes grew faster and her plunges deeper as a guttural sound began to snake its way up her throat. Pushing one finger inside, she reached down with her other hand, slathering her fingers with her desire, and then began drawing frenzied figure eights over her clit.

"Christ!" she screamed as she felt the orgasm begin. "Oh...Jesus..."

Crying out as it washed over her, Jamie stilled her hands, gasping for air as she rode out every wave, and as the tremors faded, so did the images of Diana Clarke. Taking a deep breath, Jamie opened her eyes and reached for her wine. Taking a sip, she allowed the headiness of the vintage to slow her heart, and when her pulse no longer raced and her breathing had slowed, she rose to her feet. Gathering her clothes, she decided it was time for bed. Tomorrow was another day, and she had things to do.

CHAPTER SEVEN

As she turned off the main highway and drove down a tree-lined country road, Diana's heart began to race. Since deciding not to go to Vermont for Christmas, she couldn't stop thinking about a woman with soulful eyes and an extremely kissable mouth. After spending part of her weekend shipping packages to her family, Diana spent the rest of it counting the minutes until she'd see Jamie again.

With the freshly plowed section of road barely wide enough for two cars to pass, Diana checked her mirrors twice before stopping and turning on the dome light to check the directions included with the invitation. Realizing that she only had a few miles to go, her smile widened.

Tucking the invitation back in her purse, she continued down the road, merrily humming to the sounds of Christmas coming from her radio.

A few minutes later she saw lights ahead in the darkness, and soon the trees gave way to a split-rail fence wrapped in tiny white Christmas lights. Smiling at the simplicity, and thankful for the guiding light they provided, she followed the fence line until she came upon a stone-pillared entrance. Pulling into the driveway, Diana slowed the car to a crawl as she took in the view.

At the end of the winding drive was a Georgia-style farmhouse. With the center section two stories in height and the additions on either side slightly shorter, it appeared almost as wide as it was tall. The stone house was completely outlined in white lights, and with candles in the windows and wreaths hanging on the double doors leading into the home, the decorations were as uncomplicated as they were elegant.

Enjoying the fact that Jamie's taste in decorating matched her own, Diana continued up the drive, but quickly hit the brakes when an elf came into view...a rather tall elf, at that. Amused at the sight of the gangly man dressed in a snug green and red costume complete with a red and white striped stocking cap, Diana shut off the engine as he approached the car.

"Merry Christmas, miss," he said with a bright smile as he opened the door. "I'll park your car for you."

"Oh…okay," Diana said, trying to keep her grin to a minimum. Jamie's invitation clearly stated that the night was going to be a casual affair, and when Diana stepped from the car and the cold winter air wrapped itself around her, she was grateful for the warmth her jeans, sweater and boots provided. Buttoning her leather jacket, she handed the man her keys. "There you go."

"Enjoy your evening, miss," he said, getting behind the wheel.

"Thanks."

"Oh, miss."

"Yes."

"You'll need these," he said, handing Diana the gloves she had left on the passenger seat.

"I will?"

Receiving only a wink in response, Diana watched as the elf drove away. Shaking her head with amusement, she took a deep breath of the cold night air and then jogged up the stairs to the door. Ringing the bell, she laughed out loud when she heard the "ho-ho-ho" of the chime.

Inside, Jamie had just finished giving instructions to the staff in the kitchen, and making her way up the long hallway leading from the back of the house, she broke into a trot when she heard the seasonal doorbell's message. "I'll get it, Sam," she said to a waiter dressed in an elf costume. "They've got more trays in the kitchen to bring out. Give them a hand, will you?"

"Sure thing, Miss Nash," he said as he headed down the hall.

Pausing in the foyer as a few of her guests walked by carrying plates filled with food, by the time Jamie reached the door, the "ho-ho-ho" had begun again. Chuckling at the sound, she opened the door wide and announced with glee, *"Merry Christmas!"* Shocked to see Diana standing outside, Jamie's mouth fell open. "Diana?"

Although the temperature was well below freezing, Diana suddenly felt warm...very, very warm. The sight of Jamie wearing a plush Santa cap and white cable-knit sweater adorned with festive name tag announcing she was *Santa's Helper* brought a smile to Diana's face. But it was the woman's tight black jeans and knee-high boots that captured Diana's attention...and held it. Damn, Jamie looked good.

It took a few moments before Diana was able to raise her eyes and gaze into those staring back at her. Amused by Jamie's open-mouth gawk, Diana grinned. "Merry Christmas, Jamie."

Still working her way through stunned, Jamie blurted, "What are you doing here?" and then immediately shook her head at her own words. "I'm sorry…I…I…I just didn't expect to see you tonight. I was told that Gwen couldn't make it, so I just assumed…I mean…I thought—" Stopping to snicker at her own fumbling, Jamie backed away from the door. "Would you like to come in?"

***

She sat in a wing-backed, leather chair near a glowing hearth, wiping the tears of laughter from her eyes…again. On the floor in front of her, surrounded by little girls, Jamie was attending a tea party. Although trying her best to remember which hand held her invisible tea and which held her invisible cookie, Jamie was failing miserably and Diana was on the brink of losing control of her bladder. She couldn't remember ever laughing so hard, and she couldn't ever remember feeling so good.

Shortly after she had walked into a house filled with the aroma of things sugary, spicy and festive, Jamie introduced Diana to her guests, but those in attendance had never roamed the carpeted hallways of Phelan, Willoughby and Nash.

When it had been decided that three parties would be held, Jamie saw no need to give more to those that already had so much. Sending her corporate clients baskets of fruit, to the people who had walked into her storefront office in the South Bronx, she had extended invitations on ivory parchment. Promising them a night filled with fun, food and a few surprises, she asked them to visit her home on Christmas Eve, and graciously, many had accepted.

They showed up with eyes wide and smiles bright, wearing their best jeans and corduroys. Walking through the door, they placed in Jamie's hands small tins of homemade cookies, tiny casseroles holding family favorites and ornaments made from colored paper, and their generosity had left her stunned. How could those who had so little, still smile so easily or be so gracious? How could children give her a gift, when under their trees, there would be so few?

Jamie's only wish for that night had been to give a few families a Christmas that they would never forget, but they had turned the tables on her, and she found herself humbled. She had never planned for the night to become a tradition, but as she looked up from the floor and saw Diana smiling back at her, a strange sensation washed over her. Jamie knew that Christmas Eve parties at her home *would* become a tradition, and Diana would be attending every one.

The tea party came to an end, and as the little girls scampered back to the dining room to fill their hands with cookies and candy, Jamie took a deep breath and looked back at Diana. "How you doing up there?"

"Me? I'm fine," Diana replied, looking around the room. "Although I have to tell you, I can't believe that your colleagues are the same people that I met a few weeks ago. They seem so…so down-to-earth now."

Looking over her shoulder, Jamie saw Ted Phelan sitting cross-legged on the floor with his two children, while Lillian was perched atop a stool near the Christmas tree reading a story book to a small group of toddlers at her feet.

"It's a side of them that most never get to see," Jamie said.

"And you do?"

"Believe it or not, yes," Jamie said, leaning close so only Diana could hear. "A few years back, Ted went through a rather nasty divorce, but what gutted him the most was not being able to see his kids every day. The man was an absolute mess. There were even a few nights when I had to help him get home, because he had drunk himself into a stupor over it all. Don't get me wrong, the man can be a total prick, but he loves his kids."

"And Lillian?"

"She raised three of her own, adopted one more and has six grandchildren with another one on the way. She can be as ruthless as the day is long, but her heart melts when it comes to children."

"And does yours?"

Smiling, Jamie climbed to her feet and held out her hand. "Come with me and you'll get your answer."

Sensing that Jamie's party plans for the night had not yet ended, as Diana took her hand, she said, "How come I don't think you're done playing Santa Claus?"

Without answering, Jamie simply smiled as she led Diana through the room. Coming to a stop next to where Ted Phelan was sitting, Jamie touched his shoulder to get his attention.

For a split-second, Ted sneered back at her, but then remembering his children were close by, he displayed the biggest of grins. "How you doing, Jamie?"

"Sorry to interrupt, Ted, but can I see you for a moment in the foyer?"

"Sure thing, Jamie," he said, springing to his feet. After tousling his son's hair, he gave his children strict orders to behave themselves and then followed the women out of the room. As soon as they reached the entrance hall, the sneer reappeared on his face. "What's this all about, Nash? I don't get a lot of time with my kids, so I prefer not to waste it on the likes of you."

Taking a deep breath, Jamie shook her head. "Listen, Ted. Tonight isn't about you and I, okay? It's about these kids. So I'm asking you, just for tonight, can you please just give me a break? Please?"

He opened his mouth, preparing to let fly another cutting remark, but her words stopped him in his tracks. He had expected her to return his barb with one of her own, but instead, she only asked for a bit of common courtesy, and she was asking for it on Christmas Eve. Remembering that he had just spent the last two hours in her home, enjoying a night with his children, Phelan's expression softened, and he nodded his head. "What do you need, Nash?"

Relieved, Jamie said, "Linda had to leave to catch a train, and I've got a few things I need to do before the clock strikes nine. When it does, I need you to gather everyone and get them onto the patio. Can you do that?"

"What? Why?"

Thinking for a moment, Jamie smiled. "Because, what's Christmas without Santa Claus, Ted?"

As much as he tried not to, a smile appeared on his face. He didn't like the woman. He didn't like her kind. He didn't like her intelligence, or the fact that the most beautiful woman in the room was on *her* arm, but damn it all to hell, the merriment in Jamie's eyes had just become contagious. He had no idea what she had planned, but suddenly Ted Phelan wanted to be a part of it. "Consider it done."

***

Standing on the patio just outside the kitchen, Diana took a breath of the frosty air and looked up at the heavens. Snow had begun to fall again, but unlike a few days earlier when it had rushed to the earth in whirling squalls, now it was just drifting lazily to the ground in silence. The light of the full moon found its way through the clouds, and in the misted darkness, hundreds of twinkling stars sparkled against the backdrop of night.

Lowering her gaze, she looked out across the rolling, snow-covered meadow behind Jamie's house. Appearing to go on for several hundred feet before ending at a stand of trees at the base of a hill, the only disturbance to the thick, white quilt of snow were a dozen trees dotted across the field, all of which were covered in white lights. Drawn to a brightly lit steeple atop the hill, Diana asked, "Is that a church?"

Behind her in the darkness, Jamie smiled as she stubbed out her cigarette. Walking over, she didn't stop until she was a hairs-breadth away from Diana. Looking up at the church, Jamie snickered. "No, all homes around here come with steeples."

With a snort, Diana glanced over her shoulder. "Ha, ha."

Grinning, Jamie said, "Actually, this house used to be the rectory."

"Really?"

Hunching down just a bit, Jamie pointed over Diana's shoulder. "There's a set of steps built into the hill. See them?"

Diana could see the stairs in the distance, but with the feel of Jamie's breath washing over her cheek, speaking was not yet possible. Taking a moment to relish in the closeness, she cleared her throat. "That's one hell of a climb."

"You get used to it," Jamie said as she stood straight.

"You go to church?" Diana said, turning around.

"I try to make an appearance when I can," Jamie said. "I hadn't been since I was a kid, but after I moved in here, I kept finding stuff that belonged to the church. I must have climbed those stairs a dozen times in the first week alone, and then one afternoon, the pastor showed up at my door with a welcome basket and an invitation to come to Sunday service. I figured what the hell...and I've been going ever since."

"That's nice."

"It works for me," Jamie said with a shrug.

Nodding in agreement, Diana turned her attention back to the landscape behind the house. Breathing in the chilly air, she said quietly, "This is absolutely beautiful."

"So are you," Jamie murmured.

Diana smiled, and without saying a word, she leaned back just far enough so that their bodies touched. What she was feeling was as marvelous as it was frightening, and in a whisper, she said, "Jamie, I've never felt like this before."

"Neither have I," Jamie said, resting her chin on Diana's shoulder. "I know that we've only just met, but I feel like...I feel like I did the first time I sat in that church up on the hill."

"What do you mean?"

"I've found something that I want in my life...for the rest of my life."

Diana's jaw dropped as all the air rushed from her lungs. What she was thinking Jamie had just put into words, and taking a ragged breath, she whispered, "Me, too."

With her mouth mere millimeters away from Diana's ear, Jamie purred, "I want to kiss you."

Turning around, Diana looked up at the sky for a moment. Lowering her eyes to meet Jamie's, dimples appeared as she said, "But there's no mistletoe hanging above us."

"That's because I didn't buy any."

"No? Why?"

"To tell you the truth, I was a bit...well...I was a bit pissed off when I found out that Gwen wasn't going to be here tonight. I thought you were standing me up."

"Not a chance."

"I know that now," Jamie said. Invading Diana's space, Jamie rested her hands on Diana's hips. "And I don't think we need mistletoe, do you?"

Silently, Diana shook her head. Watching as Jamie lowered her mouth to hers, Diana's eyes fluttered closed, but just as their lips were about to touch, a snowball collided with Jamie's head.

"What the fuck!" Jamie shouted. Wiping the snow from her face, she trotted to the other side of the patio to look for her assailant.

"Do you see anyone?" Diana asked with a giggle.

Scratching her head, Jamie returned to Diana's side. "No, but it was probably just one of the kids having some fun."

"And ruining ours," Diana said with a playful pout.

Stepping closer, Jamie said in a sexy whisper, "Now, where were we?"

Slowly, lowering her mouth to Diana's, Jamie's eyes closed, but then they opened wide hearing a loud, chattering chime coming from her coat pocket. "Fuck!" she said, pulling out her mobile. Turning off the alarm, she jammed it back into her pocket. "Shit!"

"What's wrong?" Diana asked.

Grabbing Diana's hand, Jamie said, "No time to explain, but I'm late. Come on."

Jamie led Diana to a set of steps at the far end of the porch. Gesturing toward a path shoveled in the snow, she said, "We've got to run. Okay?"

Clueless, but loving the spontaneity of the moment, Diana said, "I'll follow you anywhere."

"I'm going to hold you to that." Giving Diana's hand a quick squeeze, Jamie trotted down the stairs with Diana following close behind, and when they reached the path, Jamie smiled. "Try to keep up. That is...if you can."

In the second it took for Diana to register what Jamie had said, the woman was already several yards down the path, and setting her jaw, Diana sprinted after her. Trying not to laugh as she ran as fast as she could, the sting of the crisp air against her face brought back memories of sleds and snowball fights. Of brightly-colored boots and mittens fastened to her jacket with a string, and snowsuits so stiff, it was all she could do to move.

Seeing Jamie disappear behind some tall evergreens, Diana sped up, but as soon as she cleared the trees, she stopped in her tracks. Hidden behind the pines was a barn entirely outlined in white lights, and leaning on one of the doors was Jamie, playfully tapping the face of her watch.

"I wasn't that far behind," Diana said, trotting over.

Snickering, Jamie said, "I know." Pointing to the far door, she said, "Grab the handle, and it'll slide open. I'll get this one."

"Okay," Diana said, jogging to the other door. Being two-thirds the height of the barn and covered in wide planks of oak, when Diana grasped the iron handle, she did it with purpose. Tugging with every ounce of strength she had, she promptly fell on her ass when the hefty panel moved almost effortlessly. Giggling, Diana scrambled to her feet, and refusing to acknowledge the amused look on Jamie's face, she clutched the handle again. "Let's try that again, shall we?"

Easily opening her door while Jamie did the same with the other, the snow-covered ground was instantly awash in the light streaming from the barn. Filling her lungs with air, Diana peeked inside and her eyes opened wide. "Oh my God! Jamie, how did you do this?"

Wearing the largest smile she owned, Jamie said, "My sister works for an ad agency. They use it on photo shoots sometimes, but it's usually back in storage by now. I leased it from them, and…and a friend helped me with the rest."

Before Diana could say a word, a booming voice echoed through the barn. "You're late!" Turning, Diana watched as Santa Claus strode past the two white stallions tethered to the sleigh, and came to a stop directly in front of Jamie. "You were supposed to be here ten minutes ago."

"Sorry, I kind of lost track of time," Jamie replied.

Raising an eyebrow, Santa directed his attention to Diana. Eyeballing her for only a moment, he returned his focus to Jamie. Seeing that both women were displaying radiant smiles, he chuckled and shook his head. "Yes, well, speaking of time, we're running out of it. I've loaded the sacks, so climb in and let's go."

Walking to the front of the festively decorated red sleigh, he climbed onto the green-upholstered seat in the front. Adjusting the overfilled sack next to him, he glanced over his shoulder at the two women still standing near the sled. "Well, what are you waiting for?"

Taking Diana's hand, Jamie asked, "So…how'd you like to go on a sleigh ride?"

CHAPTER EIGHT

Amidst the snow flurries and darkness of Christmas Eve, and with the sleigh bells jingle-jangling as the horses trotted, the sleigh shushed through the snow. In the back seat, with a plush red and white blanket draped over their legs, the two women sat with cheeks rosy from the wind, enjoying every single second of the ride.

Diana's mind was awhirl. She had never believed in fairytales, but sitting behind Santa on a sleigh sliding over the frozen ground has a way of changing a person's beliefs. The last few hours had been filled with the smells of Christmas, the laughter of children and the charity of the season, and Diana had never felt so warm, so alive, so aware, and so much in love.

The man in the Santa costume guided the sleigh to the outskirts of Jamie's property before slowly heading back toward the house. Between the sound of the bells jangling on the horse's bridle and Santa's boisterous and continual "Ho, ho, ho," by the time they reached the house, the patio was filled to capacity.

Parents held their children's hands, preventing them from running at the moving sleigh, and the older kids, the ones who *thought* they no longer believed in Santa Claus, believed again. The snow was falling, the air was crisp, and as the clock struck nine, the bells in the church steeple began to toll. It was magical.

When they came to a stop, Santa turned to Jamie and Diana. "Okay, time for you two to hop out. I only work with elves, and you're not dressed for the part."

"You sure?" Jamie asked, quickly jumping out and helping Diana do the same.

"I'm fine," Santa replied. "Now get out of here. I've got gifts to give."

Nodding her head, Jamie winked at the man, and with her fingers still laced through Diana's, she led her away from the sleigh. In a loud, booming voice, Jamie shouted, *"Merry Christmas!"* and then watched as the overjoyed youngsters scampered down the patio stairs and dashed to the sleigh.

By the amount of children racing across the snow, Santa knew that one sack of presents definitely wouldn't be enough. Reaching in the back seat for the other bag, he jumped when he discovered that he wasn't alone. On the upholstered bench sat a little man dressed as an elf. "Where did you come from?" Santa asked.

"I'm here to help you, sir," the elf replied.

Pausing for a moment, Santa let out a hearty chuckle. "I should have known that she'd have thought of this," he said, holding out his hand. "Well, you'd best do your job, then. Start handing me those presents before the children overtake us."

"As you wish, sir," Percy said, handing the faux Santa the first of many toys in the bag. "It's what I live for."

Standing under a tall pine a short distance away, Jamie and Diana watched as the children gathered around the sleigh.

"You thought of everything, didn't you?" Diana said.

"It's just a few toys."

"No, I mean the elf."

Confused, Jamie said, "What in the world are you talking about?"

"The elf…in the back seat," Diana said, pointing to the sled.

Glancing over at the sleigh, Jamie chuckled. "I think someone's had one too many eggnogs. There's no one in the sleigh except for Santa."

With a huff, Diana looked back at the sleigh. Seeing only Santa Claus, she frowned. "I swear to you that there was a little man dressed as an elf in the back seat a minute ago."

"Of course there was," Jamie said in a placating tone. "And I suppose you see reindeer instead of horses, too?"

"I'm telling you, I know what I saw," Diana said, crossing her arms.

Seeing the change in Diana's posture, Jamie asked hesitantly, "Did I make you mad?"

"What? No, of course not."

"Are you sure?"

With a snicker, Diana said, "Trust me. You'll know when I'm angry."

Amused, Jamie said, "Well, I guess I should let you know that I've got quite a temper, too."

"Do you now?"

"Yes, thus the need for a stone home," Jamie said, glancing back at her house. "I can huff and puff all I want, and the walls will never fall down."

"Wanna bet?" Diana said with a devilish snigger. Expecting the exchange to continue, when Diana saw a broad smile appear on Jamie's face, she asked, "What's that about?"

"I was just thinking that we both have tempers, which means we'll probably have lots of arguments."

"Definitely a possibility."

"And I'll be the first to admit that I can be quite pigheaded at times."

"That makes two of us."

"So...we'll probably have to spend lots of time...um...making up," Jamie said, holding back a grin.

The frigid air had already caused Diana's cheeks to turn red, but Jamie's inference instantly added more depth to the shade. Enjoying the fact that Diana was blushing, Jamie pulled her into her arms, and as she lowered her mouth to Diana's, she said, "I think we should start practicing right now. How about you?"

The magic of Christmas Eve had allowed Percy to become visible to all, but as soon as the last sack of presents had been emptied, he had jumped from the sleigh and vanished into thin air. As he skipped eagerly to the house to deliver the last sprig of mistletoe, he saw Jamie pull Diana into her arms.

Percy was on a mission. His job was to deliver *three* sprigs of mistletoe in hopes that under one, Diana would meet her soul mate. Although he was fairly positive she already had, as far as Percy was concerned, until Diana and Jamie met under the last sprig, there would be *no* kissing.

Packing some snow into a hard, round ball, he repeated what he had done earlier that night. Winding up like a major league pitcher, he took aim and let it rip. Once again, Percy hit his target with a resounding splat, and once again, his target was *not* happy.

"What the fuck!" Jamie blurted, stumbling to the side.

Halfway between amused and concerned, Diana asked with a snicker, "Oh my God, are you okay?"

Rubbing her head, Jamie scowled and looked out across the yard, intent on discovering who had thrown the snowball. Seeing that Ted Phelan was wearing an unusually large smile, she growled, "I should have known!"

Scooping up some snow, she packed it hard, took aim and fired. Unfortunately, just as the snowball was about to reach its destination, Lillian Willoughby walked over to talk to Ted and promptly got thwacked in the back of the head.

"Oh, my word," Lillian shrieked, lurching forward.

Tickled at the sight of the dumpy woman struggling to remain on her feet, Jamie looked at Diana and shrugged. "Oops."

Having witnessed the exchange, Ted tried his best not to laugh. "Lil, you okay?"

"I'm fine," she grumbled back, dusting the snow from her jacket. "But when I find the child who—"

"It was Nash," Ted said flatly, pointing to where Jamie was standing. "See for yourself."

Narrowing her eyes, Lillian whipped around, and when she saw the smile on Jamie's face, she snatched up some snow to retaliate. A few minutes later, adults and children alike joined in on an impromptu, crazy snowball fight…started by an elf on a mission.

***

An hour later, Jamie stood at the front door of her house bidding farewell to her guests. Parents carried sleeping children to their cars, while staff members dressed in elf costumes followed closely behind with their hands filled with bags of food and gifts. Some of the invited, unable to find the words to express what they felt, offered Jamie only a smile when they walked out the door, while others embraced her, kissing her on the cheek as they thanked her again and again for the wonderful, magical night.

"So, I suppose now we should be calling you Jamie Claus, eh?" Phelan said, walking over.

Refusing to allow him to dampen her spirits, Jamie let out a long breath and shook her head. "Call me whatever you'd like, Ted. I'm used to it."

Something in the tone of Jamie's voice stopped Ted Phelan from saying another word. Stepping aside so that another family could bid their farewell to their hostess, he looked around the decorated entryway, and then down at his two children who had presents from Santa clutched in their hands. Tenderly placing his hand on his son's head, the little boy looked up and gave his father a gap-toothed smile, and taking a deep breath, Ted grinned back. Raising his eyes to meet Jamie's, he paused for a second before reaching into his pocket to pull out his wallet. Opening the billfold, he removed all the cash, folded it in half and placed it in Jamie's hand.

Confused, Jamie asked, "What's this?"

"It's for whatever they need," Ted answered, glancing around at the families roaming about. Noticing Jamie's befuddled look, he said, "Look, I'm hardly a bleeding heart, but it is Christmas after all, so just take it and use it for them. Okay?"

Stunned, Jamie looked down at the cash in her hand. Sliding it into her pocket, she debated for only a moment before extending her hand to Phelan. With a smile, she said, "Thanks, Ted."

Frowning at her attempt at civility, Ted waved away her handshake. "Don't get the wrong idea, Nash. This doesn't change anything between you and me. It's a donation, pure and simple. Don't try to read things into it that aren't there."

"Of course not. My mistake, "Jamie said, lowering her hand to her side.

"Good," he said, guiding his children to the door. "I'd better get these two home before their mom starts calling. Thanks for the party."

Without waiting for an answer, he walked outside, but stopped on the stairs when he heard Jamie call out, "Merry Christmas, Ted. Be safe."

He had spent the night in her house, playing with his children and watching as they frolicked with kids wearing hand-me-down clothes two sizes too large. He had chatted easily with the men about football, and had partaken of more than one cookie baked by women who looked older than their years. When Santa made his appearance, it had been impossible to stop the goosebumps from appearing on his skin, and when the snowball fight started, he had joined in with not one ounce of malice in his heart. It was a Christmas Eve that he would never forget, and he owed it all to the woman standing behind him. With a sigh, he let go of his children's hands and walked back into the house.

Believing that Phelan had forgotten something, Jamie stepped back to let him pass, but when he held out his hand, she cocked her head to the side in surprise. Their eyes met, and as she warily placed her hand in his, he said, "Merry Christmas, Jamie, and thanks for the wonderful night. Take care."

Before she could respond, he turned and trotted down the stairs, leaving Jamie standing at the door with a rather quizzical smile on her face. Deciding to chalk Phelan's mood up to Christmas, she shook her head and turned just in time to see Lillian Willoughby walk from the living room.

With two of her grandchildren practically wrapped around her legs, and another asleep in her arms, the woman struggled her way through the foyer wearing her usual just-sucked-a-lemon expression. Weighed down by not only the children, but two shopping bags filled with presents from Santa, halfway across the entrance hall, the little boy in her arms began to slip. Before Willoughby could react, Jamie was at her side, pulling the sleeping child from her arms.

"I've got him," Jamie said. As she gently laid the boy against her shoulder, she noticed Lillian's steely-eyed expression. With a sigh, Jamie added, "Don't worry, Lillian, I'll give him back. I promise."

Realizing that the woman was only trying to help, Lillian offered Jamie a weak grin as she placed the bags on the floor.

"I was surprised not to see your husband here tonight, Lillian. I hope he's not sick," Jamie said, watching as the staff helped the woman on with her coat.

"No, Charlie's fine, but when he saw your invitation, and it included children, he decided to sit this one out. His patience with the little ones isn't what it used to be."

"That's too bad."

"Actually, I prefer it," she said, fumbling through her coat pockets for her gloves. "This way, I have the darlings all to myself without having to listen to him moan and complain all night long. Be warned, Jamie, when husbands get old, they whine about everything."

"I'm not sure that really applies to me, Lillian, but thanks for the warning," Jamie said with a twinkle in her eye.

Realizing her mistake, Lillian's pursed her lips. Yanking on her gloves as she tried to regroup, she said, "Quite a party you threw here tonight, Nash."

"I'm sure it wasn't what you were expecting."

"That's putting it mildly," Lillian said with a snort.

With a sigh, Jamie shook her head. "I'm sorry, if you didn't enjoy yourself, Lillian. Feel free to decline the invitation next year."

Pausing for a moment, Lillian asked, "So you're planning on repeating this little Christmas soiree of yours, are you?"

"Yes, I am."

"Would you like some help?"

Jamie stared back at Lillian Willoughby as if the woman had just grown another head. Leaning in close, she said, "Excuse me?"

If there was one thing that Lillian Willoughby hated to do, it was to admit when she was wrong, but that's just what she was about to do. She had spent an evening in a home filled with the sounds and the smells of Christmas, and she had thoroughly enjoyed herself. She had read stories to wide-eyed youngsters, played in the snow with her grandchildren, and stood teary-eyed on a crowded patio when Santa had arrived on his sleigh. It had been a wondrous night, orchestrated by a woman who Lillian was now having a hard time hating. Although her views on homosexuality hadn't changed, Lillian's level of tolerance had.

"I can't speak for Ted, of course," Lillian started, straightening her posture as she took a deep breath. "But I'm getting too old to throw lavish Christmas parties for my clients. I'd just as soon send them fruit baskets and be done with it.

So, I was thinking that next year, well…perhaps…perhaps I could contribute some time…oh and money of course, and maybe help you with the party plans."

Remembering the glitz and gaudiness of Lillian's home, Jamie said, "Thanks for the offer, Lillian, but I'd prefer to do it myself. Too many cooks in the kitchen, if you know what I mean."

"Oh, oh…that's not what I meant," Lillian blurted. "What I thought is that I could put some money toward the gifts for the children, and if you needed help with the baking…or decorating, then I'd arrange my schedule, so I'd have time to give you a hand."

Mentally, Jamie quickly tallied the amount of alcohol she had consumed that night. Deciding that two glasses of wine could not have muddled her senses to a point of misinterpreting Lillian's offer, she pondered on how best to reply. It didn't take long.

"Let me get this *straight*," Jamie said, unable to prevent a grin from appearing when the word slipped from her lips. "You're volunteering to come to my home and spend *several* days decorating and baking off dozens of Christmas cookies, all the while, standing by *my* side."

"Yes, that's right."

Studying the woman, Jamie tilted her head. "Who are you, and what have you done with Willoughby?"

Not at all put off by Jamie's sarcasm, Lillian said, "Yes, well, to tell you the truth, I'm a bit surprised myself, but I'm willing to give it a go, if you are. I'm not saying that I…that I will ever change my ways about certain things, but what you did here tonight is what Christmas is all about and…and I'd like to be a part of it. That is, if you'll let me."

Totally befuddled, Jamie let out a long breath as she stared at Lillian. Thinking for a moment, Jamie narrowed her eyes. "I choose the menu."

"Of course."

"And the decorations."

"Absolutely."

"And the people *we* invite?"

"That would totally be up to you."

If it hadn't been for the fact that she was holding a sleeping child in her arms, Jamie would have pinched herself to make sure she wasn't dreaming. Her thoughts had only been to give a few needy families a Christmas to remember, but instead, Jamie knew *she* would never forget *this* day. Although smart enough to know that Phelan's sneers and Willoughby's condescending looks would reappear after the Christmas season had passed, the tiniest sliver of respect now existed between them, and if it was only to reappear each Christmas, so be it.

"Lillian?" Jamie said.

"Yes."

Grinning, Jamie nodded her head. "You've got a deal."

***

After depositing Lillian's sleeping grandson into the woman's car, Jamie bid farewell to her last guest and climbed the stairs into her house. Glancing at the staff as they cleaned up, she walked down the hallway, and stopped as she reached the library. Peering inside, she said, "You look comfortable."

Smiling, Diana looked up and then spun herself around in the high-backed, leather office chair behind Jamie's desk. "I am," Diana said with a giggle. "Nice chair."

The slightest hint of blush crossed Jamie's cheeks as she thought about what she had done in that exact chair the night before. Clearing her throat, she said, "I've got a few things to wrap up with the staff before they can leave, and then I was going to make some coffee. You interested?"

"Very," Diana said, leaning back in the chair. "I think I had one too many desserts."

"Yeah, I know what you mean," Jamie said with a smile. "Give me ten minutes and I'll meet you in the living room. Okay?"

"Sounds like a plan."

"Great," Jamie said, flashing Diana another wide grin before disappearing from the doorway.

Getting to her feet, Diana sauntered through the house, passing the few remaining costumed staff members as they carried the last of the dishes and trash bags from the dining room. Entering the living room, Diana breathed in deep the smell of pine and looked around.

Long and wide, with an enormous blue spruce at one end and an equally enormous fireplace at the other, the room was as large as it was cozy. The graceful grains of cherry could be seen in the flooring and the furniture, and the soft reddish-brown leather of the sofas and chairs added yet more warmth to the room. Strings of white lights and green garland had been draped over the windows, and the figurines of angels and snowmen sitting on the tables held in their hands small bowls once filled with candies and nuts.

Staying with the traditional colors of Christmas, the tree was filled with baubles of red and green in almost every shape and size, and threaded through the branches were hundreds of white fairy lights. Unlike Lillian's tree, with its limbs sagging from the volume of ornaments displayed, Jamie had used just enough to make it festive without being garish. Diana's eyes traveled to the angel at the top of the tree, and she couldn't help but sigh at the simplicity of the figure dressed in a white, flowing robe with a shawl of silver. She was perfect. Everything was perfect.

Hearing a noise in the hallway, Diana turned around and watched as Jamie chatted easily with the last remaining staff as they left the house. She heard the front door close, and less than a minute later, Diana found herself grinning back at the woman leaning in the doorway.

For a few seconds, they gazed at each other in silence, and then Jamie said softly, "Alone at last."

CHAPTER NINE

The silence in the room was palpable as each absorbed the meaning of Jamie's words. They were alone…completely and utterly alone.

Diana no longer had to share Jamie's attention with guests wanting to chat, or with staff members awaiting further instructions, and the reality of that fact burrowed its way through her body. As she felt it snuggle itself between her legs with a sensual thud, Diana licked her lips and took a slow, easy breath. Four weeks earlier, she had been thrown off-balance by the feelings that Jamie's kiss had evoked, but now, Diana welcomed the warm pulse of awareness deep within her body. Her fear of the unknown had been replaced by a hunger to learn. Even though she had never fallen in love before, Diana knew in her heart that she'd never fall in love again. This was it.

It had seemed an appropriate thing to say until the words had slipped from her lips, and Jamie swallowed hard at the truth of the moment. Across the room, dressed in tight jeans and a red cashmere sweater, stood the woman who, in a matter of a few short weeks, had stolen Jamie's heart. She was a woman who Jamie had kissed twice, and she was a woman who Jamie wanted to kiss again…and again. Jamie had felt lust before, but what she was feeling for Diana Clarke was well beyond that. She craved Diana like no other. She wanted every inch of her. She wanted her in every way imaginable…and Jamie wanted her for the rest of her life.

Taking a deep breath, Jamie said, "Coffee will be ready in a few minutes. I just put on a fresh pot."

"I'm not really thirsty," Diana said softly.

Worried that the evening was about to come to an end, Jamie blurted, "Oh. Um...how about tea, or maybe…maybe more wine?"

"No, I think I've had enough wine," Diana said. "I need to be clear-headed."

Jamie's shoulders fell. "Right…long drive home."

Tickled by Jamie's misinterpretation, Diana was about to clear up the confusion when she noticed something hanging above the doorway where Jamie stood. With dimples forming, she said, "You lied to me."

"Lied? About what?"

"Mistletoe."

"Huh?"

Pointing to the sprig hanging above Jamie's head, Diana said, "You told me you didn't buy any."

Confused, Jamie looked up and her eyes went wide at the sight of the spray of mistletoe tied with a red ribbon. "Where the hell did that come from?"

"Probably from a flower shop, or the mall. Take your pick."

Shaking her head, Jamie said, "Diana, I didn't buy that."

"So you say," Diana replied with a grin as she slowly walked in Jamie's direction. "But since you're standing under it, there's a tradition that we need to follow. Or am I wrong?"

Jamie's libido sprang to life, and the feel of the body rush forced a low, sexy purr to rise in her throat. Pulling Diana into her arms, their eyes locked and as their breath mingled, Jamie lowered her mouth to Diana's.

Allowing her lips to brush over Diana's for only a few seconds before pulling away, Jamie breathed in deeply and then returned for more. Anointing Diana's mouth with the tenderest of kisses, Jamie moved her lips over Diana's, applying just a hint of pressure as the woman relaxed in her arms. Heads began to tilt as flavors, new and wonderful began to blend, and with no need to rush, their kisses remained chaste until Jamie couldn't stand it any longer. Yearning to savor more, she ran the tip of her tongue across Diana's supple lips, and moaned as she was beckoned inside.

Diana had never experienced anything like this before. Her head was spinning at the sensations that Jamie's kisses were creating, and when she felt Jamie's tongue ask for entry, Diana thought she was going to die. Parting her lips, her knees weakened when Jamie slipped inside, and moaning as the woman's warm, wet tongue swept over hers, Diana answered in kind. Opening her mouth wide, she sucked against Jamie's tongue, and their kisses grew frenzied as their passion flamed.

Jamie's mind was filled with things erotic and wet. Her imagination soared at the possibilities of devouring Diana's body and juices in a whirlwind of heady sex that would last until morning, but what if Diana wasn't ready for the carnal lessons Jamie wanted to give? What if she was Diana's first woman, or worse yet…what if she wasn't?

Pulling away, she gazed at Diana as she tried to find the words, and taking a deep breath, she asked softly, "Are you...I mean...have you ever..."

With lips pink with passion, Diana offered Jamie the smallest of smiles. "Does it matter?"

In three simple words, Diana had told Jamie all she needed to know, and her heart melted. It didn't matter if Diana had or hadn't and with whom. All that mattered was here and now, and the past was the past...but the future was going to be wonderful. Shaking her head, Jamie said, "No, it doesn't."

"Then take me to bed."

"Are you sure?" Jamie asked in a hoarse whisper.

"I've never been more sure of anything in my entire life."

***

Holding hands, they walked up the stairs, and entering the master suite, Diana found herself being led toward the bed at the far end of the room.

In all of her life, Diana had slept with four men, and with each, the first night spent in their arms had been edged with anxiety. The kind of nervousness that comes from opening yourself up to someone for the first time, from letting them see you at your most vulnerable, your most tender, your most needy, but Diana wasn't nervous as she walked across the room. While it was true that her heart pounded in her chest, nerves were not to blame.

For a moment, Jamie let go of her hand, and walked over to turn on a bedside lamp. Returning to Diana's side, she reached up and ran her finger softly down Diana's cheek. "You are so beautiful."

"So are you," Diana said in a breath as she reached up and pulled Jamie's face to hers.

Diana held nothing back. Plunging her tongue between Jamie's lips, she took what she wanted without hesitation. With probing kisses that were both sensual and savage, her message was clear. She wanted all that Jamie had to give...and she wanted it now.

As she answered Diana's hunger with that of her own, Jamie's hands began to roam. Threading her fingers through silken tresses the color of the darkest of chocolates, Jamie cradled Diana's head as she continued to pillage her mouth. Her other hand traveled downward with purpose and reaching the mounds hidden beneath cashmere, Jamie gently cupped one breast in her hand. At first, her touch was light, content simply to hold and covet, but urged on by Diana's throaty moan of approval, it wasn't long before Jamie began to knead and squeeze.

When the need for air became too great, their lips separated for a moment, and that was all the time it took for Jamie to lift Diana's sweater over her head. The air in the room was cool against Diana's flesh and goosebumps appeared, but then she saw the look in Jamie's eyes. It was feral and ravenous, changing her sapphire orbs to the color of a midnight sky...and Diana's body turned molten.

Hungry for the woman who stood before her, it was all Jamie could do not to tear the rest of the clothes from Diana's body and take her where she stood. Breasts of alabaster rose and fell with every breath Diana took, seemingly begging for release from the bondage of the black brassiere, and Jamie answered their call. Unfastening the clasp, she slowly drew the thin straps down Diana's delicate arms.

Brazenly exposed to Jamie's hungry stare, Diana's nipples began to ache as they filled with need, and as Jamie leaned down, Diana's entire body began to throb.

Cupping one magnificent breast in her hand, Jamie tweaked at the pebbled bud, watching as the little point grew erect and large. Rolling it between her fingers, she listened as Diana's breathing grew louder, and then lowering her mouth, Jamie covered the tip and sucked hard.

"Oh, God," Diana said in a breath, feeling her juices flow thick between her legs. "Oh...my...*God*."

Tugging gently on one swollen nipple with her fingers, Jamie tortured the other with her mouth, suckling and nibbling until the tip was plump and stiff. Feasting on the feminine delights, she lost herself in the pleasure she was giving, and when Diana blatantly arched her breasts, begging for more, Jamie gave her more.

Diana's heart was pounding in her ears. Jamie owned every inch of her, and the more Jamie fondled and sucked, the more Diana needed. Deep inside, she could feel a stirring begin, and for a split second, she welcomed its arrival, but then her eyes flew open wide. "No," she said, stumbling backward. "No...no."

Stunned, Jamie stood straight. "What's wrong? Did I hurt you? Diana, what's wrong?"

"Wait...wait...wait," Diana said between gulps of air as she held up her hand.

Afraid that she had done something horribly wrong, Jamie became a statue. Without moving an inch, she waited for a few moments before she said, "Diana, please...please tell me what's wrong."

Shaking her head, Diana slumped on the edge of the bed, and crossing her arms to cover her nakedness, she said, "I...I'm...I'm sorry."

Hesitant, Jamie approached the bed and knelt at Diana's feet. "Talk to me," she said, placing her hand on Diana's knee.

"I can't."

"Please, if I've done something wrong, I need to know what it is."

"You haven't...You didn't...Shit!" Diana said. Hiding her face in her hands, she muttered, "This is *so* embarrassing."

Bewildered, Jamie rested back on her haunches. Staring up at Diana, she tried to think of something to say, but then she remembered the conversation they had downstairs. With the slightest of grins, she said, "Diana, I know that we hardly know each other, and I know...well, at least I think I know that this is...that being with me is probably your first time—"

"Oh, Jamie, it's not about that," Diana said, peeking out through her fingers.

"It's not?"

"No," Diana replied, her cheeks suddenly blazing with color. "Oh, I can't believe I'm going to say this."

"Say what?" Jamie asked, swallowing hard. "Please don't say you think this is a mistake."

Dropping her hands, Diana said, "No, of course not!"

"Well, then—"

Flustered, and knowing that the truth was her only way out, Diana blurted, "I almost came."

Jamie's jaw snapped shut. Furrowing her brow, she stared back in disbelief. "Excuse me?"

"I almost...climaxed."

"You almost climaxed?"

"Yes."

"You stopped me in the midst of passion...because...because you were about to come?"

"Yes."

"You don't like orgasms?"

Diana's eyes flew open wide. "Of course, I do!"

"Then I'm confused."

"Jamie, look at me," Diana said. "I'm still wearing my boots for Christ's sake, and you're...you're completely dressed. I didn't want—"

Whatever words Diana was trying to form stopped in her throat as Jamie reached over and tugged off Diana's boots. Wasting no time, Jamie did the same with hers, and after tossing them aside, she rose to her feet and quickly rid herself of the white cable-knit sweater she was wearing.

Kneeling once again in front of Diana, Jamie placed herself between the woman's legs. "Is this better?" she asked, smiling.

Diana couldn't speak. Mesmerized by Jamie's bronzed torso, she swallowed the moisture building in her mouth. Hidden behind a bra of white were breasts Diana yearned to see, and the reality of the hunger heating her blood caused her body to pulse with need.

Cupping Diana's chin in her hand, Jamie lifted it until their eyes met. Gazing into brown eyes flecked with gold, she asked, "Are you afraid of me?"

"No."

"Are you afraid of this?"

"No," Diana said, shaking her head.

"Then let it happen," Jamie said with the softest of grins as she got to her feet.

Taking a ragged breath, Diana smiled back, and when Jamie gently urged her to lie down, Diana went willingly. Their eyes remained locked on each other as Jamie removed what was left of Diana's clothing, and without denim to hold in her scent, the aroma of Diana's need rose in the air.

Climbing onto the bed, Jamie lay by Diana's side, gazing at the goddess who had captured her heart. Entranced, she ran her finger lightly over Diana's nose and across her lips, before leaning down and placing a soft kiss upon her mouth.

Sighing into the kiss, Diana's eyes fluttered closed, and as Jamie's hand traveled south, leisurely caressing one breast and then the other, Diana's breathing quickened.

Entranced, Jamie casually drew the tips of her fingers over Diana's body as she admired what lay in front her. Perfect breasts, creamy and plump, with coral centers and tips distended were there for the tasting, and that's exactly what Jamie did. Flicking her tongue over one tip, she licked and teased it until it was taut and pebbled while her hand continued its journey downward. Reaching the dark curls, Jamie ran a finger across the waves, inwardly smiling at their shortened length, and then ever so slowly, she dipped it between Diana's legs.

"Oh, God," Jamie said under her breath as the slickness of Diana's passion coated her finger. Sliding through the thickened folds with intent, when she reached Diana's center, Jamie slipped her finger inside effortlessly.

Diana's breath caught in her throat as she felt Jamie's finger ease into her, and arching her back, she opened her legs and silently begged for more. The desire to be taken – to be *owned* – had never been so strong, and as she felt Jamie begin to move inside of her, Diana moaned a raspy, "Yes."

Deliberate in her rhythm, Jamie took her time as she stroked Diana. Sheathing herself within her for only a few seconds, she then slowly withdrew her finger to lazily explore the crevices moist with want, and each time she returned to the warm center of her lover, she pushed her finger deeper. The evidence of Diana's passion coated Jamie's hand, and the perfume of her lust was intoxicating. Musky and erotic, it filled Jamie's senses, and as it did, she increased the tempo of her thrusts and Diana began to writhe.

The room filled with the sound of heated gasps as both women became lost in the rapture, and when Jamie added a second finger, instinctively Diana lifted her hips to receive it. Filling her completely, Jamie pumped the twin probes in and out, and within seconds, Diana's bucks turned frenzied. Feeling Diana's walls begin to clench, Jamie buried herself deep for a moment, before exiting and rubbing her fingertips over Diana's clit. Over and over, in and out, she worked Diana's need until she saw her grab fistfuls of the bedspread. Quickly entering her again, Jamie curled her fingers and pressed them against the bundle of nerves that would take Diana over the edge. Hearing the guttural moans rising in Diana's throat, Jamie whispered, "Come for me, darling. Come for me now."

An exquisite explosion of ecstasy washed over Diana as she felt the flood within her release, and crying out at the sheer power of the orgasm, she arched and shuddered as the climax claimed her. Wave after wave shattered her body, and giving herself fully to it, Diana's juices spewed forth.

Gently, Jamie removed her hand and listened as Diana's breathing slowly returned to normal. After a few minutes, Diana opened her eyes and smiled at the woman gazing back at her. "You're amazing."

Jamie grinned for a second, but when the ache between her legs pounded for attention, she licked her lips and climbed off the bed. With her eyes locked on Diana, she rid herself of the rest of her clothes, and then knelt on the mattress by Diana's side. "I need you," she whispered. "Oh, God, I need you."

Wasting no time, Diana rose to her knees, and lowering her eyes, took in the view. Areolas of dark pink were centered on breasts heavy and round, and nipples appearing like rose-colored pearls stood rigid at the centers. Jamie's breathing had turned harsh and uneven, and as her chest rose and fell, Diana's body tingled with the prospect of what was to come. Leaning down, there was no hesitation when she pulled a swollen nipple into her mouth.

"Oh, yes," Jamie gasped, running her fingers through Diana's hair. "Oh, yes."

Circling her tongue around the sensitive peak, Diana felt it grow harder, and capturing it between her lips, she suckled, nibbled and licked until Jamie grabbed her by the hair and pulled her away.

"You're killing me," Jamie moaned, shaking her head. "I'm sorry. I'm too close...I'm just too close."

Smiling at the fact that she wasn't the only one unable to hold back her climax, Diana pushed Jamie to the bed. Quickly straddling one of Jamie's legs, Diana said, "Tell me…show me."

The sight of Diana hovering over her, with lips swollen and hair tousled was the most erotic thing Jamie had ever seen. Her skin glistened with sweat, her face was flushed, and her breasts dangled dangerously close to Jamie's mouth. Even though Jamie needed release from the tempest building inside her, the thought of having Diana again was beyond tempting. Fighting the urge to ravish her again, Jamie reached up and pulled Diana's face down. Kissing her hard, she plundered Diana's mouth, sucking against her tongue and lips until there was no turning back. She needed Diana, and she needed her now.

Breaking out of the kiss, Jamie took Diana's hand and stared intently into her eyes. Guiding it lower, when she was within a few inches from where she needed Diana to be, in a hoarse voice, Jamie said, "Do what you want. All I ask is that you make it hard…and you make it fast."

Nodding her head, Diana slipped her hand from Jamie's, and waiting only a second for Jamie to shift her legs farther apart, Diana felt Jamie's sex for the very first time.

Diana had been aware of how her own body felt since her early teens, but in no way had that prepared her for this. Under her fingers, she could feel the throb of Jamie's desire, and Jamie's essence felt like honey as it coated her fingers. Astounding by the soaked, petal-like folds thickened with want, Diana moved her fingers where she knew Jamie needed them, and without faltering, pushed two inside.

"Christ, yes!" Jamie exclaimed, clasping her thighs around Diana's hand for an instant as she luxuriated in the sensation. Squeezing her legs hard, trying to ward off what she knew would come soon enough, a few seconds passed before Jamie relaxed and Diana was able to begin to move inside of her.

Honoring Jamie's only request, Diana embedded her fingers to the hilt and then began to thrust them quickly in and out of the woman's moist, tight center. Again and again, Diana plunged deep and hard, and matching Diana's strokes with fervor, Jamie raised her hips to meet each and every one. Gyrating against Diana's fingers, Jamie was quickly losing her mind. Ecstasy was on the horizon, and gasping for air, her bucks became wild as she impaled herself on Diana's fingers with abandon.

Her own breathing now fast and shallow, Diana watched in amazement as she drove Jamie to the place she had just visited. Starting as a tingling, distant and odd, and then changing to ripples of pleasure, soft and friendly, the climax would begin to build. But as the pleasure grows, the ripples begin to turn to waves, and inhibitions are lost as sensual tremors drive you toward screams.

Sheathing her fingers deep inside one more time, Diana curled them, and as she pressed against a most sensitive spot, she ran her thumb across Jamie's clit, and promptly sent the woman over the edge.

Throaty moans escaped Jamie's lips as her orgasm grew to a crescendo, and clasping her legs around Diana's hand to still her movements, Jamie gave in to the climax. Shuddering explosions of splendor swept over her, and squeezing her legs together, she cried out as her body released. With breathy groans, she rode out each wave, arching her hips slightly at the ebb and then relaxing as the sensation dissolved.

Awash in the aftermath of the orgasm, time seemed to stand still until Jamie finally opened her eyes. Taking a deep breath, she smiled up at the woman sitting by her side. "Are you okay?"

"Are you?" Diana said, returning her smile.

"Do you need to ask?"

With a throaty chuckle, Diana answered, "No."

Propping herself up on her elbows, Jamie studied Diana's face for a moment. "I have something to say, but I don't want to scare you."

Raising an eyebrow, Diana said hesitantly, "Okay?"

Taking a deep breath, Jamie said, "I'm totally in love with you."

Dimples appeared as Diana slowly leaned forward, and seconds before their lips touched, she whispered, "The feeling is mutual."

EPILOGUE

25 years later …

"Whatcha doing?"

Looking up from the toast she was buttering, Jamie said, "I was thinking about bringing someone breakfast in bed, but apparently they didn't stay put."

"You know I can't sleep when you're not there."

"After all these years, I would have thought that you would have gotten used to me getting up early."

"After all these years, I would have thought *we* wouldn't have to have this conversation *again*," Diana said with a grin.

Chuckling, Jamie licked some butter from her fingers. "Good point."

"I thought so," Diana replied. Looking over her shoulder, she listened for a moment to the silence of the house. "Are we the only ones up?"

"No, there was a mass evacuation just before eight."

"Why?"

"Lindsay's doing."

"Huh?"

Washing her toast down with a gulp of coffee, Jamie asked, "Which one of our children would you say is the most romantic?"

"What?"

"Answer the question."

"That's easy. Lindsay, of course, but what does that have to do with them leaving the house so early. Especially today."

"I think she arranged it so that we'd have some time alone," Jamie said, snickering. "Apparently our oldest daughter doesn't think we're getting any."

For a split-second, Diana stared back in disbelief, and then her smile grew even wider. "Little does she know."

"Yes, but I do appreciate the effort," Jamie said, watching as Diana walked over to the large center island and picked up a piece of toast.

Taking a few bites, she followed it with a gulp of coffee from Jamie's mug. Seeing no other food prepared, Diana said, "So your idea of breakfast in bed is toast and coffee? Maybe you should call Lindsay and have her give you a few pointers on romance."

Laughing, Jamie said, "That'll be the day."

Snatching the toast from Diana's hand, Jamie quickly tossed it in the trash. Opening the double-door refrigerator, she pulled out a large silver tray holding a bottle of champagne, two chilled crystal flutes, a bowl of strawberries and a single long-stemmed red rose. Placing it on the kitchen table, she turned around and grinned. "You were saying?"

Diana's face lit up, and as her eyes filled with tears, Jamie sauntered over and pulled her into her arms. Placing a quick kiss on Diana's lips, Jamie said, "Happy anniversary, darling."

"Happy anniversary, Jamie," Diana said, smiling back. "I love you."

"I know," Jamie replied with a cocky smirk. "What's not to love?"

Rolling her eyes, Diana reached over, picked up a strawberry and put it in her mouth. Sighing at the scrumptious flavor, Diana began to reach for another when Jamie grabbed her hand.

"Hey, don't I get any?"

"Sure," Diana replied, taking another and quickly eating it. "Have all you want."

A low growl escaped as Jamie bent down and kissed Diana again, but this time the kiss was anything but quick. Tender and slow, Jamie explored Diana's mouth, absorbing the flavors of strawberry, coffee and Diana. Their lips parted and met several times before they finally separated and gazed into each other's eyes.

"You're amazing," Diana said in a whisper, smiling up at her wife.

For a moment, Jamie returned Diana's look, but then a surge of déjà vu washed over her. Salivating at the memory, she unconsciously licked her lips as she stared hungrily at the woman standing in front of her.

Having been together for over twenty-five years, Diana had grown to recognize all of Jamie's moods. While she was more than familiar with the look in Jamie's eyes, there was something else lurking just under the surface, and it was that something else that had Diana worried. With a hint of apprehension, she asked, "What's going on in that head of yours?"

Instead of answering the question, Jamie walked back to the center island and went about clearing off the top. Placing the toaster, butter dish and coffee cup on another counter, she took off her black velour robe and laid it across the green-black granite surface.

"Sweetheart, what are you doing?" Diana asked, walking over to the island.

Wrapping Diana in a bear hug, in a flash, Jamie lifted her and placed her on the counter.

"Jamie, what the fuck—"

"Do you remember our first Christmas? Or should I say, do you remember the first Christmas *morning* we spent together?"

Staring blankly at her wife for a moment, Diana thought about the question, and suddenly her eyes bulged. "No!" she said, shaking her head. "Absolutely not."

"Why not?" Jamie asked, wearing her best Cheshire cat grin.

"Because…because we have children," Diana answered, immediately sighing at her own lame excuse.

"They're not here, and Lindsay told me not to expect them back until at least two," Jamie said, loosening the sash on Diana's robe.

Pushing her hand away, Diana said, "Jamie, you are out of your mind."

"Why? Because I want you…like I had you back then."

"Then let's go upstairs and you can," Diana said. "Why use a countertop when we can use a bed?"

Gazing deep into Diana's eyes, Jamie lowered her mouth and a fraction of a second before placing her lips on Diana's, she purred, "Because I want something to eat right now…and what better place to eat, than in the kitchen?"

Diana barely had time to inhale before Jamie captured her lips in a heated kiss, and lost in the moment, she opened her mouth and allowed Jamie inside. Tongues swirled and lips savored as they fed on each other's flavors in a passion-filled kiss, and Diana's vehement objection about making love atop the kitchen counter was quickly forgotten.

Over the years, they had made love in practically every room in their home, and furniture strong enough to hold their weight had done just that. They had discovered words that could make the other swoon and erogenous zones that could make the other squirm. They had made the most gentlest of love during nights that had turned into days, and in the midst of several heated arguments, they had ended their disagreement in a skirmish of torn clothes, sweat-soaked skin and gasps begging for more. They had fingered, they had tongued, and they had toyed.

It didn't matter that breasts now drooped a bit when once they were firm. It didn't matter that Jamie's blonde hair had lost some of its sheen, or that Diana's dark-brown was now highlighted with strands of gray. Laugh lines could easily be seen, and stretch marks would never disappear, but the effects of time had yet to dampen their spirit or desire. Their love was as undeniable as it was insatiable.

They broke out of the kiss panting for air, and as both struggled to refill their lungs, they gazed at each other through eyes now darkened by passion.

Diana knew that she could easily convince Jamie to follow her upstairs to their soft and spacious bed, but suddenly she didn't want comfort. She wanted raw. She wanted spontaneous and untamed; where their carnal lust would lead them to sweat-soaked bodies and screams born from ecstasy. Never in Diana's wildest dreams could she have imagined that she would spend the morning of her wedding anniversary on her kitchen counter with Jamie's head between her legs, but that's just what was about to happen.

Although neither had ever denied the other anything, it wasn't until Jamie saw Diana's infinitesimal nod that she began unbuttoning Diana's red silk pajama top. Swallowing hard as the fabric gaped open, Jamie said in a raspy voice, "Lift your hips, darling."

Seconds later, Diana found herself naked from the waist down, and when Jamie moved nearer, Diana wrapped her legs around the woman's hips and pulled her close. Their lips met in a hot and hungry kiss, and when the scent of Diana's desire rose up between their bodies, Jamie's sex throbbed.

With a groan, Jamie ended the kiss, and gently pushing Diana back until she was lying across the counter, Jamie licked her lips and grabbed the fabric of the black robe under Diana's body. Easily sliding her to the edge, she leaned over and began placing the gentlest of kisses across Diana's belly. Slowly moving her way lower, when she reached the triangle of shortened curls and placed her hands on her wife's thighs, Diana unabashedly opened her legs.

Jamie's breath caught in her throat at the sight of Diana's womanly petals glistening with need. Unable to resist, she ran a finger lightly over the swollen folds, and when she heard Diana moan in response, she leaned over and ran her tongue over her wife's moist center.

"Oh, God," Diana said in a breath as she lifted one leg over Jamie's shoulder. "Oh…sweetheart, yes."

Jamie smiled at Diana's ragged response. Breathing deep the headiness of her wife's intimate bouquet, she began slowly dragging the tip of her tongue through Diana's slick, puckered furrows, and quickly lost herself in the intoxicating flavor. Minutes ticked by as Jamie continued to draw her tongue through Diana's lower lips. Lapping at the earthy nectar as it seeped from her wife's core, Jamie was relentless in the attention she was giving every crevice as she licked, nuzzled and sucked Diana toward orgasm.

Their lives had just come full circle. Nearly twenty-six years before, Diana had found herself in the same kitchen, on the same counter and in the same position, and just as she had done back then, she raised her head and looked down just as Jamie looked up. Their eyes met...and the years disappeared. They were lovers still young in mind and spirit, who yearned for each other just as they had so many years before.

Swallowing hard at the intensity she saw in Jamie's eyes, Diana propped herself up on her elbows and basked in both the feel and the sight of her wife between her legs. Her jaw fell open as Jamie ran her tongue teasingly through her folds, and sucking in a quick breath, Diana reached down and guided Jamie to where she needed her.

Adoring the silent instruction, Jamie gave Diana what she knew she wanted. Uncovering her clit, now pearled to perfection, Jamie flicked her tongue over the sensitive nub, and a throaty groan rose in Diana's throat as her legs shuddered in response.

"Yessss," Diana hissed, arching up to meet Jamie's tongue. "Oh, yessss."

Exquisite sensations were running rampant through Diana's body as Jamie was slowly and beautifully torturing her to climax. Her arms quivered as she struggled to remain upright, but Jamie was being deliciously relentless, and with her breath now coming in short little bursts, Diana laid back across the counter. Placing her other leg over Jamie's shoulder, Diana gave in to the inevitable and begged, "Now, Jamie…oh…please…now."

Well versed in her wife's needs, Jamie had been waiting for the words to slip from Diana's lips, and as soon as she heard them, she eased two fingers inside of Diana's warm center. Filling her completely, Jamie worked her fingers in and out as she continued to dance the tip of her tongue over Diana's swollen clit. Slithering her left hand up Diana's sweat-soaked torso, Jamie covered her breast, and as Jamie tweaked the hardened nipple, she felt Diana's body stiffen with impending release.

Looking up for only a second, Jamie breathed, "Let it go, baby…let it all go."

Diana's body was no longer hers. Jamie had taken it away with touch and taste, and words and whispers…just like she always did. Surrendering herself to the splendor which Jamie had created, Diana sucked in a quick breath, managing to hold it for only a few seconds before her orgasm claimed its victim. Explosions of ecstasy rippled through her body, and crying out, she grabbed fistfuls of Jamie's robe, arching her body as desire flowed splendid from her core.

As soon as Jamie felt the inner shudders begin, she slowed her fingers. Remaining inside her wife, she blew softly across Diana's clit as she continued to tweak and roll Diana's hardened nipple between her fingers, prolonging the waves crashing over Diana for as long as she could. The sounds of Diana's husky sighs filled the room, and when Jamie saw the nectar dripping from Diana's center, she tenderly removed her fingers and began to lick it away. With each stroke of her tongue, Diana trembled and when Jamie felt Diana's legs go limp, she gently lowered them to the counter and stood straight.

Gently running her hands along Diana's legs, Jamie waited in silence until Diana opened her eyes, and as they both smiled at the other, Jamie helped her to sit up. "You okay?" she asked, wiping a few strands of hair off Diana's sweaty forehead.

Taking a deep breath, Diana nodded her head. "I'm wonderful," she purred, pulling Jamie's face to hers for a brief, feathery kiss. "I'm absolutely wonderful."

The pajama top was doing little to hide Diana's nakedness, and as Jamie took in the view, she said in a low, sexy voice, "You'll get no argument from me."

Chuckling at the amorous expression appearing on Jamie's face again, Diana said, "God, you're horny this morning."

"When am I not?"

"True."

"Do you mind?"

"You know better than to ask that."

"Well, it's been a quarter of a century. Just making sure you haven't changed your mind."

Reaching down, Diana grabbed the hem of Jamie's sleeveless white T-shirt and lifted it from her body. Slowly licking her lips at the sight of the full breasts before her, she reached out and cupped one in her hand. Running her finger over the erect tip, she smiled when she heard Jamie's breathing begin to change.

It was who they were, and it was who they always would be. They would remain forever in lust and forever in love, for theirs was a love that transcended body and mind. Theirs was a love of the soul.

***

The sound of silverware clinking against a wine glass quieted the banquet hall, and all eyes looked toward the long table across the front of the room. As voices lowered to whispers and guests turned their chairs to get a better look, a tall man dressed in a black tuxedo walked to the small podium centered on the table. Adjusting the microphone to accommodate his six-foot-four height, he cleared his throat and looked out over the crowd.

"Good evening. As most of you know, my name is Jamison Nash," he began as he scanned the room. "We are here tonight to celebrate the twenty-fifth wedding anniversary of two very special people…" Stopping, he looked to the two women sitting to his left, and giving them a quick wink, he continued, "…my parents, Jamison and Diana Nash."

Applause filled the hall, and waiting for it to end, he took a quick sip of wine to steady his nerves. Adjusting his red silk tie, he leaned toward the microphone and began to speak again.

"When we started planning this party several months ago, I was informed by my brother, Ross, and my sisters, Lindsay and Kristin, that being the oldest meant that I would be expected to come up here tonight and say a few words about our moms. At the time, I didn't believe that to be a problem, but as each week passed, and I thought about the words I wanted to say, I realized that my siblings had set me up to fail…and fail horribly, I might add. You see, what I want to say about my parents cannot be said in just a *few* words.

"I've known these two women for over twenty-three years, and while the first few years are a bit of a blur, the rest are as clear as crystal, and those are the years I'd like to talk about tonight.

"My siblings and I grew up in a home filled with more love and more laughter than you can possibly imagine. It was rare that we ever awoke without a smile on our face, and no matter how badly we may have misbehaved, when we climbed into our beds at the end of the day, our mothers were always there to kiss us goodnight and tell us how much they loved us."

Looking at his notes on the podium, he glanced at his sisters and brother and shrugged his shoulders. Pocketing the papers, he turned to look at the ones he lovingly called Mom and Mum.

"You nurtured us and you tickled us. You taught us how to tie our shoes, ride our bikes, and the difference between right and wrong. By the example you set, we learned to respect not only others, but also ourselves, and to never be afraid to ask for help...or give it. There was never a problem too small or a question too stupid, and no argument was ever settled by either of you pulling out the parental trump card."

Jamie and Diana sat with smiles on their faces, watching their eldest stand tall and handsome in a collarless tuxedo with satin piping down the edges. His hair was blond, his eyes were blue, and his voice was clear and crisp...and they were proud. Under the table, their hands were joined, and as they listened to his words, their grips grew stronger as their eyes filled with tears. Glancing at each other, they each took a breath and lifted their eyes to meet his. They could see he was proud, too.

"You spent many an evening by our side as we struggled to understand our lessons, and more than once you sat in uncomfortable chairs next to hospital beds when we decided to try to tempt gravity...and failed."

Ripples of laughter flowed through the room, and waiting while his audience quieted, he thought back to a day when he was eight years old and had fallen out of a tree he had been told not to climb. He awoke in a hospital with one leg broken and two mothers on the verge of hysteria. They had tried to hide their worry behind smiles, but the tracks of dried tears on their faces had told him the truth. He had been but a child, but he knew the difference between right and wrong, and he had wronged the two people in the world who he loved the most. It was a day, and a feeling, that he had never forgotten.

Realizing that the laughter had ended, he didn't think twice about leaning toward the microphone to continue his speech. "I stand here…I stand…I…"

Suddenly, he stopped as his voice cracked with emotion. Bowing his head, he took a deep breath and tried to stop the tears from filling his eyes, and not a sound could be heard as everyone waited for him to regain his composure. With a shaky hand, he reached for his wine, and as he took a sip, he quickly glanced over at his mum.

Jamie looked back at her son, and the smile on her face matched the love in her eyes. Mouthing the words, *I love you*, she sent him a wink, and in a flash, his nerves were settled and his emotions were under control.

Taking a deep breath, Jamison cleared his throat and finished what he had started. "I stand here tonight, the voice of your children, to tell you that we could never have asked for, wished for…or *prayed* for better parents than the ones we were given. You allowed us our identities and our independence, and we thrived in the light of your love."

Before he could say another word, applause filled the room. Grinning wide at the response, he looked over at his brother and sisters, all of whom were staring back in awe. He had done what they had thought was impossible. He had put into words what lived in their hearts.

Waiting until the clapping came to an end, he turned his attention back to his parents. "I think it's fair to say that everyone in this room would agree that you've proven that love truly knows no boundaries and what you feel for each other and what you feel for your children, transcends any word known to man. You've set an example that we, your children, will do our best to uphold, and the values and traditions that you have given us, we promise to pass on to *our* children. They will know our love. They will know our laughter…and they will know that Santa Claus *does* exist."

As he expected, laughter erupted in the room, and smiling at the sound, he waited until his audience got themselves under control.

"I see that there are some non-believers here tonight," he said with a grin, leaning close to the microphone. "I can assure you that I'm not crazy, nor am I drunk. A minute ago, I mentioned traditions, and like most families, our traditions grew over time.

"As many of you know, having attended numerous Christmas Eve parties at our home over the years, this time of the year is very special to my family. You see, twenty-six years ago today, the two women you know as Jamie and Diana met at a party given by Theodore Phelan, and it was at that party that they shared their first kiss under a sprig of mistletoe. A sprig,

I might add, that Theodore Phelan, to this day, assures us that he did not put there.

"One week later, at a party given by my sister's godmother, Lillian Willoughby, the same thing happened. My parents shared a kiss under some mistletoe that Lillian, to this day, denies ever buying."

Noticing that he had everyone's attention, he paused for a second to let them absorb what he had said before continuing. "Two weeks after that, at the first Christmas Eve party held in my home, my parents met again," he said as a large smile appeared on his face. "And as they say, the third time's the charm."

A titter of amusement rippled through the room, and glancing at his parents, his smile grew even wider at the sight of the blush creeping across their cheeks. Suppressing a laugh, he turned back to the audience to finish his speech.

"Under a bouquet of mistletoe wrapped in red ribbon, they shared another kiss…and fell in love. That sprig had not been purchased by Mum, yet it somehow ended up hanging in our house. I suppose that a guest could have brought it with them, but that's highly unlikely, or perhaps a staff member could have taken it upon themselves to decorate…but again, that doesn't really ring true. So, I ask you, who else at Christmas would bring a gift into a home as if by magic?"

After pausing for a few seconds to allow everyone to ponder the question he had posed, he finished his speech.

"Although our traditions are many, the one that we hold most dear happens every Christmas morning. As we sit around our tree opening presents, we ask our parents to tell us their story, and with smiling eyes, they do just that. They talk about chance, and about magic. They talk about potpourri, and an impromptu snowball fight. They talk about views, once staunch, that mellowed with time, and about a love that happened almost overnight, and it is a love, without a doubt, that will last forever.

"Ladies and gentlemen, I ask that you stand and applaud my parents as I request that they take their place on the dance floor in celebration of their love."

As deafening applause filled the room, Jamie and Diana stared at each other with wide-eyed surprise.

"Did you know about this?" Diana asked, leaning close so Jamie could hear her over the noise.

"If I did, I would have told you," Jamie said, taking a much-needed gulp of wine.

With a snicker, Diana said, "You know, he's just like you."

"Tall, fair and handsome," Jamie quipped, sliding back her chair.

"No, soppy and full of surprises," Diana said, taking Jamie's hand as she rose to her feet.

Smiling wide, with a twinkle in her eyes, Jamie leaned close and whispered, "You didn't seem to mind my surprise this morning."

Diana's cheeks flamed instantly, but before she could say anything else, their children approached. With faces beaming and eyes filled with tears, they all exchanged hugs and kisses, and then Jamie took Diana's hand and led her to the dance floor. As the room lights dimmed, the strings of fairy lights above the dance floor were turned on and seeing the sprigs of mistletoe hanging from each and every strand, everyone in the hall, including Jamie and Diana, laughed out loud. Shaking their heads at their children's humorous decorations, the two women pulled each other close and as the sound of silverware clinking against goblets filled the room, they shared a long, loving kiss. The music began, their eyes met, and as they swayed to the melody, friends and family watched as the two women fell in love...again.

***

Three weeks later...

Deciding to check on the staff, Diana made her way down the hallway. Entering the kitchen, she smiled at the men and women dressed as elves, and making her way to the counter, she browsed the selection of sweets before choosing a piece of chocolate from a tray and popping it in her mouth. Quickly coming to the conclusion that the staff had everything well under control, she turned to leave just as the back door opened and her son, Jamison, stepped inside.

"Christ, it's cold," he muttered under his breath as he shut the door against the wind. Pulling off his cap, he was about to remove his coat when his mother spoke up.

"What are you doing?" Diana asked.

Startled, he looked up, and draping his jacket over a nearby chair, he said, "Oh, hi Mom."

"Don't *hi Mom* me, young man," Diana said as she walked over and looked up at her towering son. "What are you doing here? You know you're supposed to be helping your grandfather."

"Well, I would if he didn't take after Mum."

"What's that supposed to mean?" Diana replied, crossing her arms and playfully glaring at her son.

Chuckling, Jamison leaned down and gave his mother a kiss on the cheek. "It means that he's as stubborn as she is."

"Who's stubborn?" Jamie asked as she sauntered into the room.

"Hi, Mum."

"Don't *hi Mum* me. What are you doing up here? You're supposed to be helping your grandfather."

Accustomed to their uncanny way of repeating what the other had already said, he couldn't help but laugh. "Yes, well, I went down as you asked, but as soon as I suggested that he might need help, he balked and tossed me out of the barn."

"Jamison, put on your jacket and go back down there," Diana said. "Sebastian's eighty years old and I don't want—"

"Darling, wait," Jamie interrupted, putting her hand on Diana's shoulder. "Dad's already told us that he's retiring from Santa duties after this year and—"

"Sweetheart, I know, but I don't want him to get hurt."

"Diana, he's been playing Santa Claus for twenty-six years. All he's asking is to go out like he came in…on a red sleigh pulled by two white steeds, and I think we should let him," Jamie said softly, giving Diana's shoulder a squeeze.

As soon as she heard Jamie's tone of voice and saw the look in her eyes, Diana knew that she had lost the argument. "Fine, but if something happens, don't come running to me for bandages."

Turning on her heel, she marched from the room, leaving her son and her wife standing by the back door, trying their best not to laugh.

"That was easier than I thought," Jamison said, smiling at his mother.

"Yes, but I'll have hell to pay later," Jamie said, grinning. "Jamison, do me a favor. Keep an eye on him, will you please?"

"Sure thing, Mum," he said, putting on his jacket.

Noticing something bulging in the inside pocket of her son's coat, Jamie asked, "What do you have there?"

"Huh? Where?"

Rolling her eyes, Jamie pointed at the lump in the fabric. "Coy is not your style, and you've never been able to lie to me. What's in your pocket?"

Thinking for a moment, Jamison reached in and pulled out a small bottle of scotch. "This."

Glancing at the label, Jamie said, "That's very high-end."

"He's worth it, don't you think?" Jamison said, trying without success to read his mother's expression.

Nodding her head, Jamie replied, "Wait a minute."

Walking across the kitchen, she opened a cabinet and pulled out a tin of cookies she had placed there earlier that day. Returning to her son, she placed it in his hands. "Tell him that we wish him a Merry Christmas."

***

Looking in the small mirror nailed to the wall of the barn, Sebastian Nash ran his fingers through his gray hair. No longer needing a wig to cover what was once brown, he pulled on the red Santa cap, adjusted the fake flowing white beard and sighed. Hearing the barn door slide open, he looked over and said, "You're late."

"Sorry, sir. I ran into a bit of bad weather."

Walking over, Sebastian looked down at the little man. "The snow stopped hours ago."

"I wasn't talking about Connecticut, sir," Percy said, smiling up at the man.

"No, I suppose you weren't," Sebastian said with a knowing grin.

Looking at the four sacks of presents stuffed into the back of the sleigh, Percy said, "That's more than last year, isn't it?"

"A bit, but the party has grown over the years, as you well know."

"It looks like in another year or two there won't be any room for me."

"They'll always be room for you, Percy, but I'm retiring after tonight. Next year, my grandson will take over the reins."

"Oh, I see," Percy said, hanging his head.

"He's a good boy, Percy, and I was hoping that you'd help him, just as you've helped me."

Pausing for a moment, Percy said, "I'll have to check, sir. There are rules I have to follow, and even though I made an exception with you, I'm not sure I'll be allowed to make another."

"That's fair," Sebastian replied. "But tonight, after the last sack is emptied, can I ask that you stay a bit longer. I asked my grandson to get us a bit of scotch for afterward...that is, if you have the time?"

A toothy grin exploded across Percy's face, and the bells on his cap and shoes began to jingle with excitement. "I'd be honored, sir," the little man said, waving his arm toward the front seat of the sleigh. "You'd best climb aboard now, or we'll be late."

"You first."

"Sir?"

"Tonight, we ride front seat together."

"Yes, sir," Percy said, snapping to attention. "*Yes, sir!*"

***

A short time later, as parents and children alike ran across the snow toward the sled, Diana smiled when she heard Jamie walk up behind her. Leaning back, they both sighed when their bodies touched, and as Jamie wrapped her arms around Diana's waist, she said, "I told you that he'd be okay."

Playfully elbowing Jamie in the ribs, Diana said, "I knew you were going to say that."

"If I hadn't, you would have been disappointed."

"True," Diana said with a laugh.

Seeing all the wide smiles on the faces of parents and children alike, Jamie said, "I don't think I'll ever get tired of this."

"You say that every year."

"Do I?"

"Yes, that's why the party keeps getting bigger."

"Do you mind?"

"Do you really need to ask that?"

"I love you."

"I know. I love you, too."

Focusing her attention on the sleigh, Jamie said, "Do you think he'll come back?"

"We already discussed this, sweetheart. Jamison will take over next year."

"I'm not talking about Dad."

"Oh," Diana said, watching as the elf handed Sebastian Nash another gift from a sack.

"Do you think others can see him?" Jamie asked.

"Our kids do."

"True, but even I couldn't admit seeing him the first time," Jamie said with a chuckle.

"I still can't believe you lied about that."

"It wasn't a big lie."

"I felt like such idiot, do you know that? There I was, being honest…and instead of admitting that you saw him too, you accused me of being drunk."

Laughing, Jamie pulled Diana even closer. "Did I ever tell you how much I love it when you get angry?"

Rolling her eyes, Diana looked over her shoulder and snorted. "So…who's picking the fight tonight? Me or you?"

The End

SNEAK PREVIEW

How does a person survive in a world
that terrifies them?

How do they learn to trust again?

GIVE ME A REASON

CHAPTER ONE

She had lost track of time as she sat in the dark listening to the noise of the night. Winter was coming to an end, but like she had done every night as the months had passed, the windows were open an inch, allowing the cool dampness to invade the room and saturate her soul. She didn't mind. She had forgotten what it felt like to be warm.

She turned on the floor lamp, the bulb flickering for a moment before the connection was made, but its brightness was lost behind a shade stained with the yellowness of age. It was used, bought second-hand like the few other necessities that took up space in the tiny flat she called home. A small couch, barely large enough to hold two people, its upholstery faded and frayed just like her, sat in the middle of the room while a mismatched chair stood desolate in a corner. Purchased for the comfort of guests, it had yet to be used except for the occasional piece of clothing dropped on its lonely cushion. Books were scattered and stacked around the room, some piles neat while others leaned to the left or right, waiting for the effect of gravity to announce itself. There was no need for a bookcase, just another piece of clutter, just another problem for someone else to clean up. There wasn't a reason for buying new. Why burden someone with your belongings when it would be so much easier to discard them when you're gone?

Going into the kitchen, she switched on the light, the fluorescent lamp sputtering and groaning as it was awakened from its sleep. Squinting at the brightness, she turned it off and took a few short steps to open the tiny fridge tucked under the counter. It was a paltry room, large enough for one, but too small for two. She liked that.

Taking a bottle from the shelf, she returned to the lounge and placed it on the coffee table, staring at its milky contents and wondering if tonight would be the night. Lighting another cigarette, she slowly exhaled and watched as the smoke floated over her head until it disappeared into the shadows. She glanced at the bottle again. Picking it up, she examined some particles that had settled to the bottom, awaiting their turn to be dissolved by the clear liquor inside. Inhaling a lungful of smoke, she carefully set the bottle down, within reach if the mood struck, but far enough away to keep it safe from harm. Opening her briefcase, she pulled out a packet of papers and took a sip from the bottle of beer she had been nursing for over an hour. As she read over the first essay, she grimaced. Her student had yet to comprehend the lessons being taught. Picking up a red pencil, she began to make notes and corrections in the margins. Taking an occasional drag from her cigarette, she worked through the small stack until all were graded and tucked safely back into her attaché.

Getting up, she went to the window to close the sash and paused for a moment to peer through the glass. Three stories above the street, she could still hear the sounds of tires against wet pavement and the occasional shout of a fond farewell as nightlife left the pubs and stumbled to find their way home. Letting out a long breath, she carried the bottles to the kitchen, throwing one away and placing the other safely back in the fridge, shaking it a few times to assist the remaining granules in their disappearance. Unbuttoning her blouse, she walked silently to the bedroom, and after tossing the shirt in the wardrobe, she pulled down the brightly-colored duvet on the bed, its vibrant hues in sharp contrast to the rest of the flat. Having spent too many nights lying awake on sheets and mattresses used by others, their bodily habits leaving stains and scents behind, this mattress and linens were purchased new. Although the sheets were now two years old and their colors were faded by washing, they still felt good to her.

As she lay in the darkness, she wondered how she could feel so lost in a space so small, but then again, she felt lost everywhere. The flat was simply a place to exist until the next day dawned, and tomorrow *would* dawn. Tomorrow she had work to do...so it wouldn't be tonight.

***

"Are you going to work all night?" he asked, stomping into the kitchen for the third time in the last hour.

"Duane, you know I start tomorrow, and I need to get my thoughts in order," she answered, looking up from her laptop.

Frowning, Duane said, "It's just that your work always seems to come first. There's never anything left for me."

"I'm sorry, but you know how I am."

"You mean a workaholic?"

"Yeah. Sorry."

"Look, I love that you're focused on this, and I love you. It's just that I've spent the last two days watching the telly, and I'm bored."

"And I want to make a good impression on my first day. I promise, once I get settled at Calloway, I'll give you all the time you need."

"I need time now, babe. I feel like I've wasted my whole weekend over here."

"Well, if I'm not mistaken, you invited yourself over here this weekend, not me."

"I didn't think I *needed* an invitation!"

Realizing she could have been more eloquent in her response, Laura rubbed the bridge of her nose, trying to think of a way to avoid yet another endless argument about her wants versus his needs.

Laura MacLeod was thirty-two years old, and although born in Scotland, she had moved to England six years earlier to take a rather lucrative teaching position at a small private academy in Surrey. She had always wanted to teach, to instill values and knowledge in youthful minds, so it was a dream come true...and the paycheck didn't hurt either. She was smart. She was young, and she was rapidly building a hefty nest egg.

During one summer break, a fellow teacher suggested that Laura join her in volunteering at a local women's prison. Although doubtful that incarcerated women would be as willing to learn as the boys behind ivy-covered walls, Laura reluctantly agreed. It was a decision that changed her life.

Having always taken great delight in educating others, it wasn't until she saw the appreciation in the eyes of the inmates that Laura realized she had found her niche. There was a profound difference between instructing children raised with silver spoons in their mouths, to enlightening women whose lives seemed to hold only despair. Before autumn arrived that year, she had left the pristine palace of expensive education, and taking a position at HMP Sturrington, Laura MacLeod entered the world of Her Majesty's Prison Service.

Laura enjoyed her time at Sturrington, as much as anyone could enjoy being locked behind thick stone walls for eight hours a day. Most of the women were eager to learn, and although there was an occasional conflict, more often than not it was just frustration on the part of the inmate. Laura could walk out of the gates every afternoon while they stayed behind, locked in their cells, with only their thoughts to keep them company. She understood that feeling all too well…that was until she met Duane York.

With a healthy bank account to back her up, Laura purchased a small home in the borough of

Barnet and spent her free time renovating and decorating it to make it her own. Visiting a local nursery one weekend, she accidentally bumped into a man carrying a shallow tray of flowers, sending him and the plants to the ground. Profusely apologizing, when she offered to buy him a cup of coffee while waiting in the queue to pay for their purchases, he agreed, and one week later, Duane York called to ask her out on a date.

Laura's attraction to Duane wasn't instantaneous, but like the flowers she planted around her house, it grew over time. He was an attractive man, a half foot taller than her five-foot-four-inch frame, and although slender, years of playing football with his mates had afforded him a workout that defined his muscles quite nicely.

It was a comfortable, slow-moving relationship, but when he had proposed to her a few months earlier, Laura was stunned. They were good together. In and out of bed, they were good together, but marriage meant love, and Laura wasn't sure she really loved Duane. She liked him. She liked him a lot, but a commitment of that magnitude needed more than just like, it needed love, so she told him no. Heartbroken and angry, he left her house that night saying he'd never return.

At first, it was odd not having Duane underfoot, rummaging through her pantry for nibbles or relaxing in the lounge while she fixed dinner. However, as each day passed, Laura realized that it was nice to do what she wanted *when* she wanted to do it. It was refreshing to open the refrigerator and still find it stocked with what she craved, and when she came home after a long, hard day, her house was exactly in the order she had left it that morning. There were no surprises anymore, and for the first week, it was a nice change, but by the start of the second, Laura began to miss having Duane around. She missed his laugh and his warmth, and the way they'd snuggle on the sofa together, watching the telly as they talked about their days. She missed making meals for two and evenings in the pub with friends, and she missed the love they made, even though she wasn't sure, at least for her, love had anything to do with it. So, when Duane called to apologize ten days after he walked out of her house, Laura accepted it and things returned to the way they were.

During those two weeks of solitude, Laura received a call from an old friend. John Canfield was the former governor of HMP Sturrington, but he had resigned his position at the prison two years before, deciding that he no longer wanted to live ten hours a day behind locked doors. Still passionate about helping those who could not yet help themselves, he had accepted a position as the director of one of the largest bail hostels in London whose primary focus was on education.

Two days after receiving John's phone call, Laura sat in a bustling coffee shop listening as the man across the table chattered on about Calloway House. Not just a hostel to spend the night, the week or the month, Calloway offered its occupants more than just a roof over their head and a curfew. With the current curriculum, the residents could learn to read, to write, to balance a checkbook and even fix a car if they so desired. It gave them hope and with it, self-worth.

Over their second cup of coffee, John explained that he currently had a staff of four full-time and two part-time teachers, but he needed someone to oversee not only them, but also the course schedules. He needed a person with focus, steadfast in their belief about what learning could accomplish. He needed someone who could follow rules, adhere to the strict guidelines set by the Department of Education and Skills, and he needed someone who would be willing to take the steps necessary in order to insure that Calloway would continue to receive funding. In other words, he needed Laura MacLeod.

When they had first met at Sturrington, although impressed by the petite woman with the green eyes and infectious smile, John believed that her enthusiasm to teach convicts would be short-lived. He could not have been more wrong. While many a teacher had turned cynical behind the stone walls and barred windows of the prison, Laura had not. She thrived on teaching those who craved to be taught. She adored her students and they adored her, and it didn't take long before Laura MacLeod became one of John's most trusted and valued educators. When funds were allocated to increase his staff at Calloway by one, John picked up the phone and called Laura.

Before they finished their third cup of coffee, Laura accepted the position, and when Duane York once again became part of her life a few days later, their already fragile relationship began to show even more cracks.

"Laura!"

Startled from her thoughts by Duane's outburst, she looked up from her notes. "I'm sorry, what?"

"You haven't heard one bloody word I've said, have you?" he shouted, grabbing his jacket. "That's just great!"

Flinching as the front door slammed shut, she sighed. "Shit."

***

After parking in an area marked For Employees Only, Laura climbed out of the car, gathered her briefcase, laptop and lunch, and turned around to gaze at the six-story building in front of her. Located on the outskirts of London, Calloway had been converted from an old apartment building to a halfway house nearly twelve years earlier. Showing its age in its architecture, the brick facade was broken up by tall, narrow windows, all of which were capped with thick pediments of stone, and along the roof line was a bulky cornice supported by brackets jutting out every few feet. Slightly ominous in its appearance, Laura took a deep breath as she headed to the entrance. Pulling open the heavy door, she walked inside.

Well aware that if Laura MacLeod had a fault, it was one based on time, John Canfield had been patiently waiting in a doorway off the entry. Watching as his new hire walked into the lobby, before she could say anything to the elderly man sitting behind the front desk, John called out, "Glad to see you could make it."

Looking in his direction, Laura smiled. Pushing six-foot-six, John Canfield was in his late fifties with very little hair left to speak of, but his cheerful personality and boyish charm subtracted years from his age. Gangly and soft-spoken, while they had only worked together at Sturrington for a short time, it was long enough for Laura to see John as more than just a friend, and only slightly less than a father.

"Sorry. Am I that late?" she said with a weak grin, shrugging her laptop bag off her shoulder.

"Only a few minutes," he said, taking the satchel from her hands. "Come on. Let me show you around."

Before starting the tour, John quickly introduced Laura to the old man sitting behind the desk. As with most bail hostels, or Approved Premises as they were now being called, several of the residents had strict curfews. During the week, it was Martin's job to keep track of who came and went, while at night and on the weekends, other retired prison officers took his place.

Rail thin and with his scraggy face displaying a two-day-old stubble of stark white hair, Martin grumbled a curt hello before looking back at the daily tabloid he held in his withered hands.

Rolling his eyes at the watchman's gruffness, John led Laura through a large doorway to the right of the entry as he explained that the two lower levels of Calloway held the staff offices, classrooms and community areas while the upper four floors housed the residents. Believing that part of their rehabilitation involved giving the women their privacy, although he and a few other employees were allowed to visit those who lived above their heads, he made it clear that unless she was invited, there was no need for Laura to travel higher than the second floor.

Nodding in agreement, it wasn't until they came to a stop just inside the doorway when Laura took in her surroundings. Three large sofas filled the middle of the room while a pool table stood in one corner with a Ping-Pong table in another. Vending machines were lined up along the back wall, and to her left, from floor to ceiling was a battered bookcase, its shelves dotted with a sparse collection of paperbacks.

Going over to it, Laura tilted her head to scan some of the titles and was surprised to see that most were fiction, and by the appearance of their covers, they had been read hundreds of times. "These have seen better days," she said.

"Yes, they have," John said, motioning for her to follow as he walked from the recreation area. "Unfortunately, most of the funding we receive has to be used to cover the cost of school books, food and salaries, so when it comes to the non-essentials, it's up to us to find them. All the books in there were either donated or left behind by someone when they moved out. Part of our job is to drum up more donations, so I hope you're ready to spend a great deal of your time on the phone."

Smiling, Laura said, "I am."

"Good."

"John?"

"Yes?"

"Where is everyone?" she asked, glancing around the empty lobby. "I know you told me that the residents had to have jobs or be in class, but I expected to see at least a few stragglers."

"Not a chance," John said, leading Laura to a corridor on the other side of the room. "Most of the women here know that we offer a hell of a lot more than most bail hostels. We're giving them a free education and a chance at a better life if they apply themselves, so most take our rules fairly seriously."

Walking down the expansive hallway, John stopped in front of a desk tucked into a small alcove. Sitting behind it was a woman in her mid-fifties with strawberry blonde hair.

"Laura MacLeod, let me introduce you to our office manager, administrative assistant and saving grace, Irene Dixon," John said. "Without her, I'd be lost."

Dismissing his compliment with a shake of her head, Irene extended her hand. "Welcome to Calloway House, Miss MacLeod."

"Call me Laura, and it's very nice to meet you. John's told me a bit about you. He says that you run Calloway, but they gave him the title."

Laughing, Irene's cheeks turned a soft shade of pink. "Oh, well, I don't know about that. I just try to do my best."

The phone on her desk rang and Irene excused herself to answer it, allowing John to continue the tour. Continuing past a few doors, when he came to one opposite another stairway, he opened it and ushered Laura inside.

"This is your office," he said, adjusting the blinds to let the sunlight wash over the room.

"Wow!" Laura said, her eyes opening to their fullest at the sight of the spacious office. About to express her delight, she stopped when the room was filled with the sound of chirping.

Quickly pulling his mobile from his pocket, John silenced the alarm. "Sorry, but I've got an appointment in a few minutes," he said, placing her laptop case on the desk. "Why don't we meet in my office at noon, and I'll introduce you to the rest of the staff and finish the tour. Okay?"

"That works for me," Laura said. "See you later."

As soon as John left, Laura returned her attention to her new office. In addition to the massive desk opposite the door, fronted by two upholstered chairs, several file cabinets filled one wall, and a small leather sofa ran along another. With the slightest hint of fresh paint in the air, Laura assumed the light mauve coating on the walls was new, and the wood flooring appeared to have been scrubbed and polished until it shined.

"I'm sorry to interrupt, but these just came for you," Irene said as she walked in carrying a vase filled with roses.

"Oh my," Laura said, blushing slightly at the amount of long-stemmed reds. "They're lovely."

"Yes, they are." Placing the vase on the desk, Irene leaned closer to inhale the fragrance, but before she could take another sniff, the phone in the outer office began to ring. "Oh, I'd better get that. Call me if you need anything."

"I will. Thanks," Laura said, plucking the card from the roses. Reading the words inside, her face spread into a smile.

Good luck on your first day. I know you'll be brilliant! Love, Duane

***

Before she left Calloway that night, John had introduced Laura to four of the members of the teaching staff, explaining that the missing part-time teacher was at his regular job, while the other full-time teacher had been unavoidably detained.

The first to meet the new department head was Susan Grant. A tall woman with blonde hair, Susan taught mathematics and accounting skills to their residents, and upon being introduced to Laura, she warmly shook her hand and welcomed her on board.

Next was Jack Sturges. An imposing figure of a man, although not terribly tall, he was broad-shouldered and brooding. He sported a flattop crew cut of salt-and-pepper hair, and adding to his menacing appearance was a jagged scar running down the right side of his face. Responsible for teaching history and languages, Laura was impressed to hear him move from Spanish to Italian to French and then to German effortlessly.

When she was introduced to Charlie Cummings, it was all Laura could do to keep her smile to a minimum. A portly man in his mid-forties, without the bright-red suspenders holding up his trousers, she feared that they would hit the floor in an instant. Hired on as a handyman, when John noticed the women asking Charlie questions about home maintenance and the like, he convinced the contractor to add teaching to his repertoire. Now, two days a week, he instructed the ladies of the house in basic home and automotive repair…and he enjoyed every minute of it.

Last was Bryan O'Neill, the youngest member of the teaching staff. Dressed in jeans and a red polo shirt, he shook Laura's hand eagerly, his grin toothy and his blue eyes smiling back at her like a puppy awaiting a treat. In charge of the classes on computer technology and sciences, Bryan had been handpicked by John when they had met at a teaching conference one year earlier. Fresh out of university and unemployed, Bryan had attended almost every seminar given that week and John had taken notice. Even though the young man's experience was lacking, his dedication to his profession was not, and before the conference had ended, Bryan had a job.

In the early hours of the evening, Laura left work, but only after filling her attaché with various reports and schedules that would keep her awake until late that night. As she grabbed her teachers' personnel files and stuffed them in her case, she wondered why she could only find five.

ABOUT THE AUTHOR

Lyn Gardner began her career writing fan fiction. In 2009, she sat down and wrote a story with no expectations other than to entertain. Three years later, at the insistence of her readers, and after listening to their praise, as well as their prods, she published her first book - Ice.

Now a multi-published author, Lyn lives in the sunny state of Florida where she enjoys playing a round of golf every now and then...that is, when her muse isn't whispering in her ear.

You can find out more about the author by visiting her website or her blog, or feel free to follow her on Twitter or Facebook...and by all means, say hello if you'd like.

Blog: www.lyngardner.blogspot.com
Website: www.lyngardner.net
Twitter: @LynGardner227
FB: www.facebook.com/#!/lyn.gardner.587

Other Works by Lyn Gardner

Ice

Give Me A Reason

CPSIA information can be obtained
at www.ICGtesting.com
Printed in the USA
LVHW041335221218
601473LV00001B/33/P